THE RANCHER'S UNEXPECTED PREGNANT BRIDE

MONTANA WESTWARD BRIDES BOOK TWO

AMELIA ROSE

CONTENTS

This book is dedicated to all of my faithful readers, without whom I would be nothing. I thank you for the support, reviews, love, and friendship you have shown me as we have gone through this journey together. I am truly blessed to have such a wonderful readership.

CHAPTER 1

*M*artha knew she needed to be patient, breathing shallow so as not to raise anyone's suspicions. Even though it was roughly three o'clock in the morning, and she was dreadfully tired after the horrible hand of fate she'd been dealt, she wasn't going to allow herself to rest even a few minutes for fear of missing her chance.

As Martha stood by the door, peering through the crack, the smell of sweat and beer heavy in the air, she listened intently to the sounds around her. She could hear the drunken older man on the bed beside her snoring softly, thankfully too drunk to do with her what he had paid Max for, having passed out before anything could happen. So drunk that she'd been able to shimmy off his clothes and assemble her disguise, plotting her escape the moment she'd successfully changed her outfit.

Martha listened to the bar room below, silence seeming to ring out. She could still see lantern-light from the bar itself, and she wondered if Max was still awake, perhaps counting his money from the busy Saturday night. Martha knew she would eventually need to make a move, before being forced to do unimaginable things with complete strangers. With that thought in mind, she decided the chance to escape was now.

Martha quickly opened the small room's door and stepped outside into the hallway, closing the door firmly behind her. She kept her breathing calm as she started towards the stairs that led down into the bar room. After that, she'd just have to pass the bar and get out the front door without anyone noticing her.

Wearing oversized boots, Martha stepped carefully down the stairs, being sure not to make too much noise. She wore a large cowboy hat, hoping the rim would cover her face when she bent her head down. Her long auburn hair she'd rolled and fitted into the hat, hoping the burnt orange strands of her hair wouldn't betray her. The jeans she wore felt like two tents strapped around her legs, secured only by a belt she'd fiddled with to fit her hourglass frame. The western shirt she wore tucked into the jeans was thankfully big enough to hide the fact that she was a woman. All in all, Martha felt she fitted in with the type that had come into the saloon that night, and she hoped no one would think twice about her leaving.

When Martha finally made it to the bottom of the stairs, the stench of the place was that much stronger, and her breath quickened when she noticed a few drunken patrons passed out at a few tables, barely visible from the single lantern left alight in the saloon. She skirted around the bar room as best she could, careful not to bump into any chairs or tables, her bright blue eyes scanning the room constantly in the dim light. As

Martha made it from that room towards the main bar, her eyes darted to the front door, although not before spotting a satchel on the bar.

She knew she should just make a run for it. No one seemed to be awake, and she didn't know how long the drunks in the bar would be asleep before waking. Surely the older man upstairs would be furious once he realized he didn't get his money's worth. But Martha couldn't deny her curiosity: she made two quick steps to the bar, peered into the satchel, and, confirming the contents, slung it over her shoulder and made due haste to leave the place behind.

Not being very familiar with the small town she'd been taken to, Martha didn't stop to check anything out. With only the full moon to guide her, she marched past the last few buildings on the main street and followed the road heading out of town. No matter where the road took her, no matter how long she had to walk to reach the next town, it would all be better than the hell she'd just been dumped in by the man she thought she loved.

CHAPTER 2

*G*ray Jenkins sat at the breakfast table with his bosses, Sam and Lucy Slater, and the two other ranch hands, Jensen and Tom. When Sam had put in an ad for a mail-order bride, Gray never thought Sam would attract someone like Lucy, someone strong-natured and not afraid to speak her mind. It was Lucy who started the tradition of having meals in the ranch house, giving Gray a break from serving everyone in the bunkhouse. Lucy was sure a good catch, with her black hair and piercing, stormy eyes. Not that Sam wasn't a good-looking gentleman, but Gray had never had much faith in the concept of mail-order brides. The thought alone made him smirk at the irony of it all.

"So, Gray, have you received any interesting letters lately?" Sam Slater asked with a small smile, taking a rather large bite of his food. He'd be rushing off into town to manage his office and no doubt long list of clients. Being the only doctor in town, Sam always had plenty of patients.

"Not recently, no," Gray responded carefully. His response nevertheless caused smirks and small escapes of laughter to commence. It was no secret that Gray was well acquainted with the women in the area, and that it was never difficult for him to find company for an evening. But at the age of forty-five, and after seeing how happy Sam had become after marrying, he knew that he had better give marriage a chance before it was too late. "I'm sure if they could accompany the ad with my photo, there'd be no shortage of responses."

"Don't ya worry, Gray. Your many other amiable qualities are sure to attract a large response to your ad," Jensen said carefully, trying to imitate the sophisticated way Gray often spoke due to his British heritage. Since Jensen was an old-timer, his quip was that much more humorous, causing everyone, include Gray, to laugh.

"I appreciate your support, old man," Gray returned as he slapped Jensen on the back.

"I would say you're not far behind Jensen," Tom pipped in, a man in his mid-thirties with often disheveled brown hair.

"And I'd watch your words there, my boy, because I can still run laps around you any day of the week," Gray responded quickly, causing Tom to focus on his food because he didn't want to get on the wrong side of his boss. While Sam Slater was the owner of the ranch with both steers and sheep, it was really Gray who ran the operation, and both Jenson and Tom knew that.

Lucy's sweet laughter rang out over the banter before she said, "Ye've always been a charmer, Gray. Just be honest in yer letters and I'm sure it won't be hard for ye to find a bride."

Gray smiled as he turned his gaze upon Lucy. "If I can be

as lucky as Sam in finding a bride like you, Lucy, then I'll be doing just fine."

"Oh, there ye go pulling on me heart strings," Lucy replied as Sam reached over and squeezed his wife's hand. Ever since they'd discovered three months ago that Lucy was expecting, she'd been overly emotional and quick to shed a few tears. Gray noticed the way Lucy's eyes teared up as she gazed into her husband's, and he hoped that one day a woman would look at him like that. Most of the time women just looked at him with lusty eyes, and though he enjoyed an evening with company, Gray wanted more in his life than just a string of one-night stands. It was time he found his one and only.

After breakfast, Sam headed out of the door after embracing his wife, while Tom and Jensen got to work on the ranch. Having been a cook himself, and knowing that Lucy was expecting, Gray took a few minutes to help Lucy clean up after breakfast. After what she'd endured last year, he'd become slightly protective of her as well.

"Thank ye, Gray, for all yer help. Greta comes by every once and again to help me tidy up on days I just don't feel that great, but I think I'm starting to regain some of me energy again," Lucy said as she washed the dishes and Gray dried them.

"It's no trouble at all," Gray said.

Lucy regarded him: a tall man with onyx eyes and broad shoulders that made him intimidating to those who didn't know him. His handsome, angular features and the dimple in his left cheek were quite arresting. Though his dark brown hair was peppered with grey, he was no less alluring to the female kind.

"Gray, yer going to make a woman very happy. Ye work hard here on the ranch, and if yer willingness to help is any indication of how ye'd treat yer wife, I don't think ye have anything to worry about, despite yer past pursuits with women," Lucy spoke up.

Gray smirked as he looked down at her. "I think your emotions are going to your head," he quipped as he finished his task and picked up his duster from the peg by the door.

"Yer just afraid to show a woman yer soft side, Gray. All ye know is how to swoon a woman. Now ye'll have to learn to win over her heart," Lucy called from the kitchen, not bothering to follow him out the front door but just hollering away. She just didn't feel up to it today.

Donning his grey cowboy hat as he pulled on his duster, Gray stepped out into a spring morning, the bitter cold of winter finally seeming to have left Spruce Valley, Montana. The rising sun felt warm on his face as he made his way towards the barn. He could almost smell spring's fresh fragrance on the wind, though the wildflowers had yet to start rising. It had been ten years since he came to this valley, joining Sam Slater five years ago when he started up the ranch business that Sam knew nothing about. It was Gray's knowledge of steers, paired with the late Ernie Red-Dog's experience with sheep, that had made the ranch so successful. And with Ernie being killed the year before, his son Drake had thankfully taken over the task of watching over the sheep herd down the road on his own little homestead.

While Sam focused on being a doctor, Gray managed the ranch. He enjoyed the solitary work that kept his body in great shape. But sometimes he did feel lonely of a woman's touch, even though it was something he could easily seek after. But would a woman honestly consider him for a husband? He was older, lived in a bunkhouse, and though he had saved much of his fortune over the years he wasn't all that sure what a woman would expect of him as a husband.

Gray sighed as he got to work, more intent now on making repairs to the outer fence than worrying about a potential wife. After all, he hadn't received any responses to the ad he'd put in the paper four weeks ago. Perhaps he finally had to settle for the fact that he'd never marry, never have kids, and simply grow old and lonely as a ranch hand, much like Jensen had done. Putting on an emotionless mask as he was skilled at doing, Gray cleared his mind and saddled his horse, focusing only on his work.

CHAPTER 3

our weeks on the road had done Martha good. After making it to the first town when she successfully escaped hell, Martha had been able to rent a small room at an inn, and with the help of the inn owner, Betty, Martha had been able to recover and regain her strength. Once Martha had rested, bathed, and purchased a horse and riding clothes, she'd taken to the road again, intent on getting as far away from Wisconsin as possible.

Martha knew that travelling alone on the open road was dangerous for a woman. That was why she carried a small pistol in a saddlebag that hung on the front of her saddle, in close proximity to her in case she'd need it real quick. And though she was always on watch for other travelers on the road – or worse, the men she was running from – Martha was enjoying traveling and living on her own.

Granted, Martha had been on her own ever since she was nineteen when her father had passed away, leaving her a small ranch in Wisconsin. After selling all the cattle, Martha had taken work as a waitress at a small restaurant, enjoying the social aspect, though she disliked smelling like food all the time. And with it being a small town, Martha knew everyone, and knew that there were no eligible gentlemen in the area. That was probably why she fell so hard and fast for Jared.

He had been like a breath of fresh air in an old, dusty town. He came in for a local rodeo and quickly won her heart with the sweet nothings he whispered in her hair as he held her, promising a better future as his wife, a life on the road as they went to rodeo after rodeo. It sounded like an exciting life to Martha, who saw no future of her own. And it didn't hurt that Jared was a handsome man with light blond hair, sparkling blue eyes, and a body like a god. Martha had been shown many aspects of Jared's body, and had become intent on marrying him. And though he had shown her passion like she had never known, with his steamy kisses and the gentleness with which he made love to her, Martha now knew that it had all been a ploy to destroy her.

She pushed the disturbing thoughts from her mind as a town appeared on the horizon. She urged her mare into a canter, intent on making it to the next inn before dark. Having passed into Montana a few days ago, she worried less about being found by her ex-fiancé and the devil of a man he'd sold her to, and started to think more about her future. She was tainted in terms of marrying material. She'd be considered "spoiled goods" to any gentlemen. So she was intent on reinventing herself and getting away from the bad memories of her past.

Martha approached the town of Helena and found it to be a

bustling place. She'd never seen a place so big and was thrilled with the possibilities this town could hold for her. She felt her confidence return to her as she rode down the main street at a trot, looking at all the shops and stores in the setting sun and finding the local inn easy enough. With her mare, which she'd named Chestnut after its coloring, situated in the local livery stable, Martha took her saddlebags towards the inn.

"Good evening, my dear. How can I help you?" asked a young gentleman when she entered the inn and approached the check-in counter. He was tall, with light brown hair and deep blue eyes. Though he appeared charming, he was the type of man Martha now stayed away from. And by the way his eyes roamed over her figure, she knew she'd have to be as lacking in charm as possible in order not to give this guy the wrong idea about her.

"I'm looking for a room to rent for the night. I'll be wanting a hot bath and dinner to be brought to my room," Martha said sternly, with little warmth in her voice as she narrowed her eyes at the man.

The man seemed startled by her reply and stammered, "Certainly. Can I get a name for the reservation?"

"No," Martha replied with little hesitation.

"Oh, I see," the man stammered again, trying to figure out how a woman as beautiful as she could be so cold and demanding. Yet the man recognized the type: this was a woman who was running from something. "I have a room upstairs and could have our housekeeper assist with the bath and dinner."

"I'll take it," Martha replied in turn, looking forward to

setting down her saddlebags and being able to unbraid her long hair. When the man told her the total cost, Martha fished out a few bills and passed them across, causing the man to raise his eyebrows. "That's for the room and your discretion," she explained as she took the key and made her way upstairs without a look over her shoulder.

As soon as she was in her room, a pleasant and clean space with a connecting water-closet, she dropped her bags on the ground near the four-poster bed and started pulling her hair from the long braid. Though the braid made it more comfortable for riding, she often preferred her hair down and flowing freely. Just as she was done with her hair, a knock came at the door. With an eye on the saddlebag that held her pistol, she moved towards the door.

"Who is it?" Martha called through the door.

"Cynthia, ma'am. I've brought you a dinner plate," called a woman from the other side of the door.

Martha unlocked the door and opened it a crack, confirmed that Cynthia was who she said she was and that she was alone, and then opened the door all the way to let the woman in. Cynthia was an older woman, her hair pulled back into a tight bun, most likely the most comfortable arrangement for her type of work, and set the plate on a nearby table. The aroma alone made Martha's stomach rumble.

"I'll let you enjoy that for a bit, and then I'll have Freddy, my nephew, bring up the tub. I'll have hot water along in no time." Cynthia chatted away, her kind eyes putting Martha at ease.

"Thank you, Cynthia," Martha replied in kind, sitting down next to the table, her mouth watering at the sight of fried chicken steak and mashed potatoes. Riding all day always made her hungry, especially when dinner was her largest meal of the day, and being alone, she rarely worried about table manners, despite the way she'd been raised.

"My pleasure, my dear. I've also brought the daily paper in case you fancy something to read," Cynthia said as she set the paper down next to the plate of food, before leaving the room.

Martha rose swiftly and locked the door, then sat again to devour her food. The taste was divine for such a simple dish, or perhaps she'd simply been that hungry. After she'd finished and wiped her mouth and hands, she turned to the newspaper, happy to have something to do till Cynthia and her nephew returned with a tub.

She flipped through the pages, noting the local crime reports and pleased to see that things seemed calm around the area. She read through a few ads for employment, but found nothing that suited her, which was fine for the moment since she still had quite a stash of money to tide her over. With a smirk on her full lips, she then read over the mail-order bride ads. She always found them amusing – and sometimes sad, when an ad sounded desperate.

As Martha glanced through the paper, she couldn't deny that a certain mail-order bride ad had caught her eye. The author was an older gentleman, a ranch hand who lived in what sounded like a quiet town called Spruce Valley. Martha smiled at the description of the man. "I look better in person," the ad read. Martha was curious to know why a man with stable employment and good humor hadn't found a wife already. She wasn't about to give her heart to someone again, but perhaps someone to live with, someone who could offer her protection, would be worth marrying in any case. She'd certainly not make the mistake of falling in love. She couldn't risk that kind of heartache again.

Though Martha had never heard of Spruce Valley, the fact that the town was in Montana seemed like fate had dealt her a good hand. Surely, she couldn't be that far away. When a knock came at the door again, and she was able to confirm the identity of two on the other side, she allowed Cynthia to enter along with her nephew, Freddy, who carried the tub with little effort. But despite his good looks, and obvious strength, Martha didn't have eyes for him at all, which seemed to please Cynthia. And once the older woman had the tub filled, she left Martha alone once again, saying they'd return in a bit to remove the tub.

After ridding herself of the riding dress, petticoat, shift, and boots, Martha slowly eased herself into the hot water, letting out a soft sigh. The water helped her sore muscles relax, which was much needed after several days of riding. She took the time to wash her hair, ridding herself of the grime of the road. She felt pleasantly clean by the time the water started to cool.

As she soaked in the tub, her mind drifted back to the mail-order bride ad. She thought of what the author might look like, what the body of an older gentleman of forty-five would look like after working so many years as a ranch hand, helping to raise cattle for his employer. After daydreaming about the author's features, Martha pushed the fantasy out of her mind. She instead focused on the logical aspects of such a match. Protection, security, a decent income ... yes, these were the only sensible aspects of marriage, because she knew from experience that true love didn't exist.

As Martha got out of the tub and dressed in an evening gown, not quite ready for bed, she found writing paper in a nearby desk and started penning a response to the ad. Surely it wouldn't hurt to write back and perhaps secure some sort of decent future for herself. Not wanting to ever be discovered by her past, she signed her letter Mary Carter instead of Martha Walters. Indeed, the Martha of the past was truly dead. Now she could be whomever she wanted, as long as it allowed the demons of her past to stay there.

When Cynthia and Freddy came to collect the tub and dump the water, Martha handed Cynthia the letter, along with a bill, asking for it to be posted first thing in the morning. Cynthia had the same reaction as the young man downstairs who had checked her in. Her eyes grew large and she nodded her head several times.

"Yes, ma'am, I'll make sure this gets posted at sunrise," Cynthia said with a curtsey before leaving the room. Martha smiled as she locked the door for the last time tonight. She was happy to surprise these people with the large tips she gave them. She felt like she was doing some good with a horrible man's money.

With nothing left to do, she readied herself for bed and brought the newspaper with her as she blew out the lanterns in the room and got under the comforter. She spent some time outlining the ad with her finger, and memorizing the words. She silently prayed that this Gray Jenkins would turn out to be her savior from the horrors of her past. Or at least provide her with a better future.

CHAPTER 4

"Gray!" Sam called from the parlor as soon as the man walked through the doorway for the evening report.

"I'm coming, I'm coming," responded Gray as he hung up his duster by the door before strolling into the parlor, sitting in his favorite wing-back chair by the fireplace, removing his pipe from his pocket and preparing it for an evening smoke.

"You know, I don't think I like the idea of you smoking in the house with Lucy expecting," Sam said casually, looking at the ranch hand that was in many other ways very gentleman-like.

Gray gave Sam a curious look as he lit his pipe, took a long draw, and let out the smoke. "And why is that, Sam?" he asked, his brows knitted together.

"Well, you know. The smoke isn't good for the baby," Sam reasoned.

This made Gray chuckle as he pointed the pipe at Sam.

"My friend, I'm not blowing smoke right into Lucy's or the baby's face. Lucy isn't even in the room," Gray countered, rolling his eyes at the thought of how protective Sam had become of Lucy ever since he confirmed she was expecting. His retort caused Sam to cross his arms in annoyance.

"Fine. But I hope this lady doesn't mind that you smoke," Sam said, changing the subject as he withdrew a letter from his suit pocket and handed it to Gray. The older man puzzled at what Sam was referring to as he took the letter and analyzed the elegant hand in which the letter was addressed to him.

Gray didn't know what to think of the letter. First, he was surprised that someone had actually written to him. Second, the address came from the inn at Helena. It made him wonder what the woman had written about, and if this woman was someone he had been with before. He'd been with plenty of women, from Spruce Valley to Helena, and wondered if someone he had been with had recognized his name from the paper and had decided to try to play husband and wife with him.

"Well, aren't you going to open it?" Sam pushed, as curious as Gray about what the letter contained. Gray ignored him for a minute as he took off his cowboy hat, set it aside, and ran his fingers through his hair.

"It's addressed from Helena," Gray started, flipping the letter over and then back again as he looked at the delicate way the letters had been written.

"I did see that. I didn't think your ad would run this close to town," Sam said, seeing how this could be a possible disaster given Gray's womanizing ways in the round-about areas.

"Nor did I. What if it's from someone I know?" Gray wondered out loud as he placed his pipe in his mouth and used both hands to open the letter carefully.

"Only one way to find out," Sam said as he moved forward on his chair.

Gray finished opening the envelope and pulled out two sheets of writing paper.

DEAR GRAY,

I hope you don't mind my informal greeting. I figure since this isn't a business letter, I didn't need to be so formal. My name is Mary, and I'm not originally from Helena. I originate from a boring, small town in Wisconsin that I put behind me earlier this year in pursuit of something a little more exciting than a life as a waitress at a stinky restaurant. I love cooking food, I just hate smelling like it.

I've been travelling on the road these past four weeks, trying to find a new place to settle down and grow some roots. I found your ad in the paper and decided it wouldn't hurt to write since it seems that Spruce Valley isn't that far from Helena, and I figured it could be a decent place to check out. Though, as your ad stated, Spruce Valley is also a little town, I've come to find that any new place is a lot more exciting than the place I used to live. And with no family left, I'm free to roam and go wherever I'd like. However, travelling on the road can get very tiring after a while, and I look forward to being settled once again.

To give you an idea of what I look like, I have what they call an hourglass body. My hair is auburn, and very long. My eyes are blue, and I've been told are quite bright in the sunlight. I have a mare whom I've named Chestnut, who seems to enjoy being on the open road and has been a great companion these past few weeks.

I'm competent in all things domestic and would make any man a good wife, but I'm looking for someone who is more mature and knows what they want in life. Though I'm twenty-nine, I'm not worried about our age difference in any aspect. As a ranch hand, I'm sure you're fit enough to take on a woman like me.

Well, that's enough of that. If this letter interests you at all, reply. Whether or not it leads to anything, I plan to stop through Spruce Valley in a few days just to see what it's like.

Sincerely,

Mary Carter

GRAY SMILED as he folded the letter back up and tucked it into his jean pocket, turning his attention back to his pipe. Sam looked at him from the edge of his seat, clearly on tenterhooks. This made Gray smile even wider as he let out a puff of smoke.

"Come on, man. What did the letter say?" Sam demanded, though careful not to raise his voice too loud to disturb Lucy in the other room. She'd come down with a headache and he didn't want to wake her with his outburst. But he was dying to know what was in the letter.

"I don't think Mary would appreciate it if I shared all her details with another man. But either way, I'm sure you'll get to meet her soon," Gray responded cryptically, enjoying torturing his employer.

"What? What does that mean?" Sam said, wanting to throttle the man. "At least tell me something about her."

Gray thought about it for a moment, taking his pipe out of his mouth and tapping the contents onto a nearby ashtray that Sam kept just for him. "She has a mare named Chestnut," he settled for, smiling wickedly as he stood.

"For Pete's sake, that's not what I meant," Sam protested, crossing his arms and leaning back into his chair like a scolded child.

"That I know, my good chap. Now, if you don't mind, I have a letter to write to Miss Mary," Gray said as he stood, donned his hat, and made his way towards the front door.

"But what about the evening report?" Sam called. The only response he got was the sound of the front door shutting, and Lucy calling down the hallway for him to stop shouting. With a heavy sigh, Sam stood and made his way to the bedroom and his wife. He was intent to rid her of her headache and tease her about Gray's letter from this Miss Mary. Sam knew that what little information he had been able to get from Gray, his wife would learn tomorrow after breakfast.

CHAPTER 5

"Calvin' time is right round the corner," Jensen said the next day between bites of lunch. The men were seated on the front porch of the ranch house, eating sandwiches that Lucy had prepared, along with fresh lemonade.

"I agree, Jensen. I feel like any day now it will be a round-the-clock watch on the herd," Gray agreed before taking a long sip of his drink. He wanted to get back out in the pasture and start counting how many cows were currently expecting, and then meet up with Drake and Robert, the shepherds down the road, and see how many extra hands they were going to need this season with the newborn lambs.

"Sounds like ye fellows are going to be extra busy these next few weeks," Lucy piped up as she came onto the porch and offered them some oatmeal cookies she'd made that morning. Lucy seemed to be craving the sweet treat, since she'd made some every day that week.

"Right ye be, bonnie lass," Gray said, imitating Lucy's

accent. Though she didn't look it, Lucy was Irish through and through, but her accent had diminished over the years.

"That will be quite enough of that, my good sir," Lucy replied, giving Gray a taste of his own medicine. Tom and Jensen laughed at the bantering before thanking Lucy for the meal and heading back out towards the pasture.

Gray got up to follow them, but Lucy asked, "Are ye going to tell me about her?"

Gray sighed heavily as he put on his grey hat. He should have assumed Sam would say something to his wife. Gray fixed his onyx eyes on Lucy, standing well above her, as he said, "Only if you do me a favor first."

Lucy smirked as she crossed her arms over her chest. "And what kind of favor are ye asking of me?"

Gray shrugged his shoulders, trying to act casual about it all. "If you take my letter into town and have it posted, I'll tell you the little I know about Mary during supper," he offered, his smile growing as he watched Lucy roll his eyes at him.

"We have a deal, ya bloke," Lucy responded, flashing her eyes at Gray as though she'd gotten the better end of the deal. Little did he know that Lucy already had plans to go into town and get more baking supplies. She also wanted to take some cookies to Greta to thank her for her help during the beginning of her pregnancy.

Gray chuckled as he handed Lucy the letter he'd written last night in his bunkroom. And with that he stepped off the porch and made his way towards his horse, intent on finishing his tasks before super. He also wanted a distraction from thinking too much about Mary. He had so many questions and was hoping to soon get some answers, either through their correspondence, or perhaps in person.

Lucy looked over the letter as she readied herself to go. Tom had already promised to have the buggy ready for her, so all she needed was her beaded drawstring purse and grocery basket before she was set. She wished she could open and reseal the letter so she could learn what Gray had written to this mysterious Mary. Lucy could only hope that Mary was someone who could do Gray some good, provide him the type of happiness she'd found with Sam. With that happy thought she set out towards the barn, Gray's letter safely tucked in her basket.

~

Dear Mary,

Thank you for your letter. I found it both interesting and amusing, and I'm glad you already feel comfortable being less formal in our letters. I can imagine you riding the open roads, your auburn hair glowing in the spring sunshine like a beacon. I'm sure when you come to Spruce Valley, you won't be hard to spot. When we meet, you'll be able to hear my British accent, something I could never hide even if I tried to.

I'm glad to read that you don't particularly mind our age difference. Let me reassure you that I'm quite fit and able for my age. With that being stated, I want you to know a bit more about myself than a simple ad could describe. Everyone who knows me can tell you I'm charming, humorous, and, quite frankly, was a womanizer. The last bit I used to be proud of, but now that my life has progressed and I've seen the way Sam and Lucy are happy together as a married couple, I've learned that there is more in life than just a warm body to hold at night.

I know the best way to form a business relationship is with complete honesty, and I'm sure that it works the same way with a romantic relationship. I want to be completely honest with you as we move forward. I'm a great romancer, but have little experience in the relationship department. However, I'm a very committed man and would never cheat on you if we started courting. I might have a tainted past, but I've always been a gentleman.

Now I have some questions for you. I find it interesting that you've been roaming these past few weeks, and though you've stated you're just looking for a new start, that usually means something happened in the past to cause a person to leave what was familiar. I don't mean to pressure you by reading between the lines, but let's just say that with age comes wisdom. I've done my share of roaming and know what it's like. Let me just add that you can tell me when you're ready.

I look forward to meeting you, Mary, and getting to know each other. Because frankly, you can only learn so much about a person through letters. Let me know when you'll be passing through town and I'll come to meet you, and even invite you out to the ranch to meet everyone. Calving season is approaching, and I'll be extremely busy keeping an eye on the herd in case any of the cows are going to need assistance with the birthing. It's quite a special time of year, to be honest.

Well, that's enough for now. Till next time,

Gray

. . .

MARTHA READ and reread the letter a handful of times before setting it aside on the table in her hotel room. Her emotions ran the gauntlet as she thought of what Gray had stated. He sounded charming and alluring in his description of her and in the fact that he had a British accent. When he wrote about his past with women, it made her stomach clench. She didn't want to end up with someone who was going to be with other women behind her back. But she figured that might be the case if she was never able to give her heart completely over to a husband. And then, when Gray hinted at the real reason behind her travels these past few weeks, she knew that he was a very intelligent man.

At first Martha didn't know quite what to do about his letter. She was intrigued by Gray, for sure, but would he understand her past as much as he was expecting she'd accept his? It seemed that if he was going to be open and honest with her, then she should be the same with him. What she knew for sure was that this wasn't something to discuss in a letter. And with Gray giving her the opportunity to talk to him about her past when she was ready, she felt less pressured.

Martha picked up the cup of tea she'd had delivered to her room after lunch and took a sip, already thinking about her response to Gray. She was enjoying the lemon tea when a strange feeling took her. She set the teacup aside and rested her hand on her stomach, worried that her lunch wasn't settling well with her. And when the pain became unbearable, she stood and moved quickly to the water closet, her stomach contents coming back up again. After a few minutes, Martha washed her face and walked slowly back to her chair, hoping the sickness would leave her. She started to think that it was time to move on.

After pausing here for a few days, she was itching to get back on the road. She'd spent the last week cooped up in the hotel room, not wanting to be spotted by anyone who might know Jared or Max. She had gone to the general store very early in the morning, just to stock up on some necessities she'd need while travelling; but she'd taken all of her meals in her room, and now she was feeling a little antsy.

Moving over to the writing desk, Martha pushed back her long auburn hair, which she'd allowed to flow freely when she was alone in her room. There was no need to put it up when she had no plans to socialize with anyone. Taking out a sheet of writing paper, she began constructing her response to Gray. Within an hour of posting it, she planned to make her final arrangements to get back onto the road. And by the time she arrived in Spruce Valley, Gray would have received her letter, no doubt.

"Time to take a chance on a better future." Martha spoke to herself as she began writing. Though she felt bad for using a false name when Gray had been so honest about his past, Martha was at least confident that she would tell Gray the whole truth about herself before they tied the knot. Her stomach fluttered at the idea of being married before the end of the year, but she knew that anything was better than being sold as a slave to be a saloon girl.

Martha managed to finish the letter before her nerves got the better of her. The moment it was sealed, she made her way down to the front counter to have it posted and to announce that she was leaving the inn.

"You'll be sorely missed," the young man replied on hearing Martha's announcement.

"How can I be, when I was never here?" Martha replied with a wink.

"Of course, miss," the man said with a nod of his head.

And with that she returned to her room, changed from her day gown into her riding clothes, making sure to braid her hair for the journey, and gathered her saddlebags to make the trip to the livery stable to collect Chestnut.

The moment Martha was on the open road again, heading to Spruce Valley having received directions from the stable boy, she finally felt like she was able to relax. Away from the town, and the increased population, she felt free and in control of her life.

"Spruce Valley, here I come!" Martha called to the wind, the sweet smell of spring on the air as the wind whipped by her as Chestnut galloped down the road. The sun was still high in the sky, and she knew that by the time the day ended she'd be closer to hopefully settling down for good.

CHAPTER 6

*S*cruffy barked as he noticed a familiar rider coming up the lane to the homestead. He barked a few times and ran over to his owner, Drake, letting him know that they had company. After taking Sam up on his offer, Drake had remained on his late father's property, turning what was once a shepherd's shed into a decent homestead. Now Drake looked after a decent-size herd of sheep with Scruffy, assisted by his younger brother, Robert, and his sheepdog, Monty.

"Good day, to you," Gray called as he neared the pasture where Drake and Robert stood carefully watching the flock, particularly a group of ewes that the sheepdogs had separated from the rest of the herd, no doubt keeping an eye on them just like he and the other ranch hands were keeping an eye on the cows for newborn calves.

"Hello, Gray," Drake said, approaching the pasture gate as Gray dismounted his horse and flipped the reins over the fence. Drake, the eldest, was a serious, taciturn young man, but he possessed keen intelligence and a kind heart. He and his brother were of mixed heritage, their father being a descendant of the Crow Indian tribe, not too far from town. It was their father, Ernie, who had taught Sam all there was about cattle drives, taking care of steers, and even a herd of sheep. It had allowed Sam to diversify his income when being a doctor alone couldn't pay the bills, and thankfully it had allowed Gray a stable job. Now both of Ernie's sons took care of the sheep operation while Gray focused solely on the steers.

"I've come to see how the lambing is coming along," Gray explained as he hopped the fence and joined the men in the pasture. Drake was impressed by Gray's agility for an older man. He smirked as he turned his eyes to the few lambs that had already been born.

"Things are good here. The weather is warmer than we expected, so the late nights are not so terrible. Sometimes March can be very bitter this time of year, making the birthing season that more difficult," Drake said, knowing that Gray would carry his message back to their employer.

"We are feeling the same way with the cows. But we know that it has just begun. Sam and I are wondering if you two will need any more assistance out here, especially at night," Gray stated, looking out over the sheep and glad he was only responsible for the steers. He couldn't imagine assisting in the birth of such small animals, especially when the sheep would need shearing soon after the lambing season was over.

"We have been taking turns." Robert spoke up. "And our sheepdogs do a good job of letting us know if any of the ewes are stressed out." Drake was the more softly spoken one, always getting straight to the point, whereas the younger brother Robert was more outspoken and a lot chattier. "Drake's been watching over the herd most of the night and I've just come to relieve him. I don't think we'll need any more help."

Drake regarded his brother for a second before turning his dark eyes back on Gray. "I agree with my little brother that at this time things are manageable. But we'll let you or Sam know if that changes," he said, his tone stern.

"I have no doubt of that, my dear fellow. Good luck to you, then. I best be getting back to the ranch. I don't mind leaving Tom to watch over things, but sometimes Jensen worries me," Gray admitted as he walked back to his horse, Drake following after him.

"Jensen is getting older. But with no family of his own I doubt he'll retire," Drake reasoned.

"I have the same fear," Gray replied, hopping back over the fence and mounting his horse. Gray gave Drake a nod, who grunted in return before he turned his horse back towards the lane that joined the main road. Gray was glad to hear that Drake and Robert were having no trouble with the sheep this year, but he wondered if he and Tom would be having difficulties with the new calves, especially since it was true that Jensen was just getting too old to be a ranch hand anymore.

By the time Gray had made the hour-long trip back to the ranch, the sun was already setting. Once he'd put his horse away in the stable, having brushed the stallion down and filled his food bag, Gray made his way towards the ranch house, hoping that dinner was still in full swing.

"Well, it's about time you showed up," Sam said good-heartedly as Gray came through the door, hung up his duster, and pulled off his hat, setting it on the peg over his duster.

"The work never seems to end at this time of year," Gray retorted, and sat down next to Tom at the dinner table, quick to fill his plate with the pot roast Lucy had made. "Looks amazing as always, Lucy."

"Thank you, Gray," Lucy replied in kind. Gray couldn't help but smirk when he noticed an oatmeal cookie beside Lucy's plate.

"How are Drake and Robert holding up?" Sam asked once Gray got settled at the table.

"They seem to be doing just fine. When I told them about the offer of an extra hand, they declined. It seems those two are just like their father. I'm sure glad Drake took up your offer instead of heading out to California to chase some gold-digger's dream," Gray said before taking a few large bites of his food. He was famished, but knew he still had a long night ahead of him.

"I agree with you one hundred percent on that. I wouldn't have known what to do if Drake had decided to leave last August like he intended to. And the fact that his brother has joined him with watching over the sheep – why, I feel quite lucky that fate has dealt us such a good hand," Sam said as he reached over and squeezed Lucy's hand. She smiled back at him before pushing her plate away and eating the cookie. Gray dared not comment on it since he didn't want to hurt Lucy's feelings, but he couldn't help but smile at the scene.

"What's got you all smiles over there, young man?" Jensen said, seeming to catch on to what Gray saw and looking for a way to poke fun at him, as he often did.

"Oh, just thinking of boss man and his misses. What a great pair they make," Gray quipped, not willing to take Jensen's bait tonight. Jensen rolled his eyes as he turned his attention back to his food.

"That's so sweet of ye, Gray," Lucy said, tears in her eyes as her emotions started to get the better of her. At this point Gray was trying to contain the bubble of laughter that was threatening to spill over. "I know that before too long you'll have a special someone in yer life, too," she added.

Gray just nodded his head, unable to speak, but his mirth was immediately squelched when Jensen stood and quickly left the ranch house, not bothering to take his plate to the sink as was his custom. Gray watched him go and then sighed, guessing what was irritating the old man.

"What's got into him?" Sam asked, standing to go after the older man. Gray raised his hand to stop him.

"Sometimes Jensen gets like this, especially during the calving season," Gray explained as Sam sat back down at the table. "Jensen has no family of his own. No wife. No children. Don't think he's not happy for you and Lucy, because he is. But I'm sure sometimes he regrets not going after a wife like he has steers all these years. Cattle drives is all Jensen knows, and I'm sure he wished he knew about the other fine things in life as well as a good day's work." It wasn't hard for Gray to say these things, for he felt the exact same way. There was silence around the table as everyone reflected on this.

Eventually Tom got up from the table and bade the others a good evening, saying he was going to go watch over the herd tonight. Gray just nodded his head in agreement, knowing he'd relieve him in a few hours. Gray now took the opportunity to speak to his employer about what Drake had spoken about earlier.

"Though Drake and Robert are doing fine this lambing season, I think it wouldn't hurt to hire another ranch hand for the steers. I'm afraid Jensen isn't cut out for this type of work anymore. He can't assist with the birthing, and he can't stay up all night like he used to. I'm not saying let him go, because God knows that man has nowhere else to go. But it might be time we started looking for someone else to help out around here," he said in all seriousness.

Sam let out a deep sigh as he looked over at Lucy, knowing that Gray spoke the truth. He was sure the re-evaluation was going to pull at Lucy's heart-strings, and he could see the tears in her eyes. Lucy pushed back a lock of her black hair, trying to hide the fact that she was rubbing the tears from her eyes.

"I can talk to Josh about it in the morning. I'm sure the Sheriff will have a recommendation for us. I would hire Grant again if he hadn't taken up the position of assistant deputy, but I'll have to think of someone else," Sam said as he started thinking about who might be able to help out, if only temporarily. He could check in with one of the Murtaugh brothers, Eddie and Sawyer, and see if either one of them were in need of a job. The brothers often acted as deputies for Josh, but now that the Sheriff had a full-time deputy, Sam wasn't sure what the brothers were up to nowadays.

"I'll leave that to you, boss," Gray said as he rose from the table. He took the dishes to the sink, bade the couple a good night, and putting back on his coat and hat, made his way out to the bunkhouse.

Gray wasn't surprised when he entered the building to see darkness behind Jensen's door. He was sure the old man wanted to be left alone. Gray went to the lantern hanging in the common room and blew it out before making his way to his own room. Stripping down to his long underwear, he fell into bed, knowing that a few hours of sleep would do him good and help him make it through another night. Though he hoped that Sam could hire another ranch hand before too long, Gray's mind was now filled more with thoughts of Mary.

He knew it wouldn't be too long before they actually met in person. He felt reaffirmed in placing a mail-order bride ad after watching Jensen this evening, when the other man's bitterness got the best of him. Gray knew that Mary might be his only shot at finding a wife since he hadn't received any other letters, which wasn't surprising considering his age. But after telling Mary about his past with women … he only hoped he hadn't scared her away.

Gray sighed, closing his eyes tight, and praying that some day he'd be as lucky as Sam when it came to finding a great wife.

CHAPTER 7

*A*fter the two-day ride to Spruce Valley, thankfully with no more sickness, Martha was excited to see what the little town was all about. Leading Chestnut down the main road at a slow walk, she eagerly looked around. There were a few establishments that lined the main road, the largest being Frost's Mercantile, according to the sign that hung out over the front porch. Martha led her horse over to this establishment, curious to see what she'd find inside.

Stepping in through the front door, Martha took her time looking over the goods, pleasantly surprised to find the store both very tidy and containing a large variety of items she wouldn't have expected in a small town. It was undeniably a lot better than the little store she was used to back in Wisconsin.

"Can I help you look for anything?" a large, middle-aged man with graying dark hair asked as he approached her.

"No, sir. Just looking. But I do smell something rather

heavenly," Martha said as she looked past the man to what seemed to be a small restaurant at the back of the store.

"Indeed, and you'll find more than one thing delicious at the Eatery. Emmet and Ella are great cooks, and Nell's a fantastic waitress. You can't go wrong," the man enthused, seeming very pleasant.

"Why, I do appreciate the recommendation, Mr …?"

"Frost, and this is Frost's Mercantile, which I manage with my wife," the man explained. "And you might be?"

Martha couldn't help but smile at Mr. Frost's way of turning the conversation back to her. "My name is Mary Carter," she said slowly, the name still unfamiliar to her tongue. "I've just arrived from Helena and I'm quite famished."

Mr. Frost regarded the young lady, her beautiful auburn hair done back in a simple braid, allowing her bright blue eyes to shine without hindrance. Mr. Frost couldn't remember seeing her before, and since he knew all the families in the area he was quite curious about Miss Carter's sudden appearance.

"And what brings you to the little town of Spring Valley? I hadn't realized that the stagecoach had already run today," Mr. Frost said as he gazed out the window. His shop also served as the local depot, so he was always the first in town to meet newcomers.

"I rode in on my mare, actually," Mary explained with great confidence. She pointed to Chestnut outside, her reins wrapped around the fence post.

"My goodness, I've never heard of a lady travelling that far on her own," Mr. Frost exclaimed.

"Fear not, good sir. I'm hoping to make Spruce Valley my new home. There is a certain gentleman I've been corresponding with that I also hope might become my husband," Martha said in a soft tone, giving Mr. Frost a wink.

Mr. Frost chuckled, as he understood Martha's reasoning. "A mail-order bride, then?" he said, to which Martha nodded in reply. "Well, then, let me be the first to welcome you to Spruce Valley. Perhaps I could give you directions so you can go meet your intended?"

"Perhaps," Martha replied simply as she gave the man a smile before moving past him to the restaurant. She wasn't about to give away such sensitive information, since she wasn't even sure that her letter to Gray had arrived yet. She didn't want anyone knowing she was here to meet him and perhaps tip him off that she'd arrived. No, she'd rather he came to her.

Martha settled down at an empty table, pleased to see that the restaurant wasn't too busy. A woman who she could only assume was Nell approached the table. "What can I get you, my dear?" she asked as she handed Martha a menu.

"Could I start out with a cup of tea?" Martha asked as she opened up the menu.

"Certainly," Nell said, and turned from the table. It appeared to Martha that Nell wasn't the most social, and after her own years of experience working as a waitress, she knew that personality was a big part of the job. She also didn't bother looking over the menu, intent as she was on getting Nell's recommendation because the waitress always knew what was best.

Martha gazed around the room looking at the other

patrons. She never felt uncomfortable eating in a new place because she never stayed in one town or another for very long; but since she hoped to make Spruce Valley her new home, she couldn't help but feel curiosity about the other patrons. Surely after a while she'd come to know everyone in town, much like she had when she was a waitress in Wisconsin. She watched those around her, trying to imagine what their stories were.

When Nell returned with a teapot and cup, Martha was impressed by her pouring of the tea, which seemed to be quite a ritual. "Your tea-pouring skills are quite impressive," Martha commented as she picked up the cup of tea, taking a small sip.

A smile came to Nell's face as she regarded the new girl. She'd never seen the woman before and was curious about her. It was rare that ladies came to dine at the Eatery alone. "Thank you, ma'am. Now, do you know what you want to eat?" she asked.

"What would you recommend?" Martha asked, delighted by the taste of the tea; it was perhaps the finest cup of tea she'd had in as long as she could remember. Martha could imagine herself coming to the Eatery for the tea alone.

Nell seemed pleased by Martha's question, given the way she smiled enthusiastically. It was like a new person had magically appeared in Nell's place. Martha could instantly tell that Nell appreciated being asked for once, instead of told. "Well, Emmet made an excellent meatloaf today that I would highly recommend. And Ella baked a fresh apple pie this morning. It smells heavenly back there," Nell enthused.

"Well, then, that's what I'll have. Thank you," Martha replied.

Nell stuck out her hand. "My name's Nell," she said.

Martha returned the woman's gesture, shaking her hand. "Mary Carter, pleased to meet you."

"The pleasure's mine," Nell replied, and then hurried away to place her order. Martha smiled as she sipped her tea, glad to have met two new people in such a short time since arriving in Spruce Valley.

By the time Nell had returned with a plate of meatloaf and mashed potatoes, paired with a small plate of pie, Martha was quite famished. Trying her best to be ladylike, she dug into her food, not evening noticing that someone had taken a seat at the table next to her and was watching her with amusement. It wasn't until the young man cleared his throat that Martha looked up and realized she was being watched.

"I beg you're pardon," she said as she picked up the napkin and dabbed her full lips. "I didn't know I had an audience."

"Was my fault. I shouldn't have been staring," the man replied with a smile. Martha observed the man for a moment as she took another sip of her tea. He had rather sharp features, and his warm brown eyes held intelligence. She then noticed the lawman's badge pinned to the front of his western vest and could only assume the man was either a deputy or the sheriff himself.

"It's rude to stare, you know," Martha replied, taking a bite of the apple pie and closing her eyes for a moment as she enjoyed the sweet taste. But this only caused the young man to laugh at her. She narrowed her eyes at him then, being rather put out by having her meal interrupted.

"I'm so sorry," he said as his mirth subsided. "You're quite right about me staring, but it's not to often that Spruce Valley sees any new young women in town. I was simply curious, and then amused that someone as petite as yourself could eat that much."

"I don't know if I should be offended or take that as a compliment," Martha replied as she turned her focus back on her pie, trying to enjoy the rest of her meal.

"Sheriff Josh Ryder, at your service, ma'am," the man finally came out with. He tipped his Stetson towards her and she nodded in return.

"Mary Carver," Martha replied, becoming accustomed to the new name.

"Well, Miss Carver, what brings you to this fine little town?" the Sheriff asked. Martha figured it was only his job that caused him to be so curious and nosey, and therefore she couldn't fault him for that. After all, it wouldn't hurt to befriend the local Sheriff if she did run into trouble in the future.

"I'm looking to start fresh in a new town, and I've been corresponding with a possible husband-to-be," Martha explained, finally finishing her pie.

The Sheriff's brows rose at this news, followed by him leaning forward and whispering, "And who might the lucky fellow be?"

Martha couldn't help but chuckle and lean forward as well, whispering back, "You'll have to wait and find out." The look on the Sheriff's face made her laugh: he was obviously put off by her response.

Nell came by then and took the Sheriff's order as Martha laid a few bills on the table, knowing it would cover the cost of the food and then some. Martha stood and nodded towards the Sheriff before she made her way out of the restaurant, waving at Mr. Frost as she left the general store. Her next goal was to find the local inn and get some rest, the great meal already causing her to feel exhausted.

As JOSH WATCHED the young lady with fiery auburn hair leave the Eatery, he couldn't help but think that whoever the man was who was going to be her husband was a very lucky man. Mary was beautiful, for sure, with her shapely figure, her piercing blue eyes, and a look about her that just seemed wild. And the witty way in which she spoke to him made him tingle all over. He couldn't wait to meet a woman like her one day.

While Josh was enjoying his food and speaking with some of the locals who had come in for lunch as well, he was pleased to see Dr. Sam Slater come into the Eatery. Josh wanted to discuss the matter with someone who might know which men in town were currently looking for a mail-order bride, and since Dr. Slater knew everyone in town, and was a close friend of his, he was certain Sam would know.

"Sam, come join me," Josh called out, waving his hand in Sam's direction.

"Thanks, Josh. How's the day going?" Sam asked as he took a seat at the Sheriff's table and quickly gave Nell his order, who went off to the kitchen without another word.

"It's been pleasantly quiet these last few days. But I have a feeling that might all be changing as I just met this fiery young lady a moment before you walked in. Did you notice her as you walked in." Josh asked, folding his arms over his chest as he watched for Sam's reaction – a habit of his.

"No, Josh, I didn't see who you were talking about. I just popped in for a quick bite to eat before I get back to the office. Mayor Delphine is coming in for her physical and I don't want to keep her waiting if I can avoid it," Sam explained.

"You're a smart man, Sam. I respect Mayor Delphine for everything she's done for this town, but she can get after you if she needs to, if you know what I mean," Josh said with a chuckle.

"That I do know," Sam replied.

"So, do you know any men around town who are currently writing to a mail-order bride? This Mary Carver explained that she was looking for a new start and had been writing to someone she called a 'possible husband-to-be'. That sounds like a mail-order bride to me," Josh said.

Sam choked on his glass of water as he listened to Josh. The Sheriff had to lean over and slap his friend's back a few times till the coughing subsided. "Did you say her name was Mary?" Sam asked as he wiped his mouth on a napkin.

"Yeah, she said her name was Mary Carver. Do you know her?" Josh asked, knowing that Sam had met Lucy through letters.

"I don't know her, but I do know that Gray Jenkins has been writing to a Mary and said that we might be meeting her soon. Gray hasn't shared a whole bunch about her, but I didn't think she'd be arriving so soon. Gray didn't say anything about it," Sam explained as their food was served.

After he'd thanked Nell, Josh asked, "Do you think Gray even knows that Mary is in town?"

Sam shrugged as he dug in to his food. "If he doesn't, he will soon enough, I'm sure."

Josh just nodded his head in agreement, digging into his own food, loving the taste of the meatloaf. Josh wasn't much of a cook, so he often came to the Eatery to enjoy a good hot meal. As he ate, he thought about Mary, and why she might be looking for a new start. Surely the woman had some sort of past. And if she was willing to come all this way to marry Gray, someone Josh knew was much older than him and Sam, then surely Mary must be desperate. In any case, Josh thought Gray was a very lucky man.

CHAPTER 8

Martha checked into the Honeywell Inn, having been welcomed warmly by Bill Eckert, the owner. The inn wasn't very large, with only four rooms to rent, but it was a neat and clean place with a decent-sized dining room, and Bill explained that her room had a water closet attached. Bill was very proud of this fact, enthusiastically talking about how his place was the only one in town that had indoor plumbing.

"I surely appreciate the consideration," was the only thing Martha could think to reply to this charismatic young man. Bill was tall and appeared to be a few years older than her. He had wavy brown hair that was parted to the side in a stylish way; his deep blue eyes were something a young lady could get lost in, and Martha wondered why this man, who ran a successful establishment, wasn't married yet.

"Certainly, Miss Carver. If you need anything, don't hesitate to come down and ask. My apartment is just down this hallway, and dinner will be served later this evening. Mrs. Royal will be by later this evening to check on you. She's quite a friendly older woman, a widow, so don't be surprised if she talks a mile a minute," Bill explained as he handed Martha her room key. She found his character assessment amusing, considering how fast Bill was talking now.

"Thank you, Mr. Eckert," she replied as she picked up her saddlebags from where she'd placed them by her feet when she'd checked in, and now, with them slung over her shoulders, she made the journey upstairs and to her room at the end of the hallway.

Martha was pleased to find her room comfortable and clean. She dropped her bags at the end of the bed: a decent size for a small room. Martha peered into the water closet as she stretched her arms, glad she wouldn't have to walk to an outhouse to relieve herself in the middle of the night. This March had been thankfully warm, but she still didn't want to be outside at night in a new town. Anything could happen in a small town like this.

For the first time in a long time, Martha felt a sense of excitement in her. She knew that whether or not she hit things off with Gray she was going to stay in Spruce Valley. She settled into a wing-back chair near the window where she could look down on the main street. She thought about how long she'd been running, and since she hadn't run into anyone from her past in the past four weeks she was starting to believe that perhaps she didn't need to worry about her past any longer.

Martha turned her gaze towards her saddlebag with all the money in it, and the other with the pistol. Though she hadn't seen a bank yet, she knew she'd have to find a safe place for her things. Staying at the inn would be a temporary option until she could either find a small apartment to rent, or perhaps an empty house to buy. She started daydreaming about the type of house she would one day want when her eyes began drift shut, and soon she was snoring softly in the chair.

As soon as Sam finished with his patients for the day, he debated whether to run home and tell Gray about Mary, or head over to the Honeywell Inn, where she was no doubt staying, and inquire of her himself. Knowing that the second of the two choices would be too forward, and would possibly land him on Gray's bad side for butting into his personal business, Sam settled for preparing his horse, Atlas, for the journey home. Once he had Atlas out of town, he set the draft horse at a fast pace, eager to get home and share the news of what he'd discovered from the Sheriff.

When Sam arrived at his ranch, he was lucky to find Gray coming in from the pasture on his own horse, looking worn out. Sam followed him into the barn, intent on getting Atlas settled quickly in the hope of having a word with Gray before he went to get some rest in the bunkhouse.

"How's it going today?" Sam called as he followed the man out of the barn. It was obvious that Gray was in a hurry.

"Had to assist two cows, and it was a long and grueling process. I thought for sure I was going to lose a momma at one point, but she pulled through in the end," Gray said in a grave voice, obviously exhausted.

"Well, I think you should rest up for a few hours and then head into town for dinner. I hear Bill is making something special tonight at the inn," Sam said with a smile. Even though Gray was exhausted, he knew his foreman would perk up at this news.

"Until you get us another ranch hand, I won't be leaving till birthing season is over," Gray said with a direct look at Sam as the man followed him into the bunkhouse, irritating him further.

"But what if I knew that a certain young lady by the name of Mary would be dining there tonight and would no doubt like some company from a certain fella?" Sam said, enjoying Gray's reaction as the man spun on his heels and looked at him with wide eyes.

"What do you mean? How do you know it's my Mary? Did you talk to her already?" Gray asked without taking a breath. He felt he had come alive again at the mention of the young woman.

Sam chuckled as he placed his hands on his hips. "I never though I'd see you get this wound up over a woman, Gray."

"Enough jerking me around. Tell me what you know, dammit," Gray said, getting annoyed again.

"Calm down, man. All I know is that a woman had lunch at the Eatery today before I got there, and Josh introduced himself to her and she introduced herself as Mary Carver, saying she was new in town and had been writing letters to be a mail-order bride. I can only assume she's staying at the inn, and since she ate at the Eatery she probably won't be going there again tonight," Sam explained as Gray ran his fingers through his hair.

"That's a lot of assumptions considering you didn't talk to the girl yourself," Gray said as he started to pace the floor of the bunkhouse, unsure what his next move should be.

"Well, I know we've been stretched thin here, but I want you to take the night off. Get some sleep, then head into town. I'm sure I could help Tom and Jensen while you're away," Sam offered, the words coming out of his mouth before he had really thought about them.

"You? Help out at the ranch? No offence, Sam, but you'd probably just get in the way," Gray said with a smirk, not believing what he'd just heard.

"I'm a ranch owner, I should know something about cattle and get some hands-on experience from time to time. I'll bring a chair out with me and Lucy can watch me mingle with the cattle. I'm sure she'll find it amusing," Sam said, wanting to include his wife. He was always keen to keep an eye on her since she was expecting.

"Have it your way, boss. I'm just glad to be having a night off. That, and I can't wait to hear about Tom and Jensen's reaction when you step out with them," Gray said as a rumble of laughter overtook him.

"Laugh all you want, Gray, but I bet I could surprise you," Sam said as he shook her head and left the bunkhouse. As the two men parted ways, Sam couldn't help but look forward to the experience, and the looks on everyone's faces when he explained to them what he was up to – and, equally important, what Gray would be up to this evening.

CHAPTER 9

*M*artha was startled by the sound of someone knocking on the door. She was surprised to have fallen asleep in the chair and quickly smoothed back her hair, and, as she rose from the chair, her skirt, too, to look more presentable. Habit caused her to call to the person knocking, and when an older female voice replied, Martha cracked open the door.

"Hello, dear. I'm Mrs. Royal. But you can call me Greta. I have some lovely jasmine soap for you if you care to have a bath," the woman said. Martha smiled and let the woman – tall, thin, with green eyes – into her room.

"Thank you, Greta, that would be lovely," Martha said as she took the soap from the woman and shut the door behind her. Greta began fussing around the room, taking the saddle-bags towards the wardrobe.

"Do you have anything that needs to be pressed or laundered?" Greta asked as she unclasped the first bag. When she peered into it, she let out a gasp. Martha looked up from where she'd set the bar of soap in the water closet, to see Greta looking into the saddlebag that contained all her money. Martha moved swiftly towards the woman and took the bag from her as she watched Greta's face flush.

"I'm so sorry, ma'am. I'm just so used to helping young ladies get settled in, I didn't even think to ask," Greta said quickly. Martha knew there was no point in getting angry with the woman since she already seemed so embarrassed.

"Please, Greta, you did nothing wrong. Here, let me show you the dresses I have that could use a good wash," Martha said as she set the saddlebag in the wardrobe and turned Greta's attention to the bag that contained her few dresses. She hadn't travelled with much, intending to purchase what she needed once she settled down.

Martha spent the next few minutes unpacking her things with Greta. She couldn't remember the last time she had done so, and it felt divine to think that she soon would have a place of her own again where she could put away all her things and never have to worry about moving again. She felt more determined than ever to find a place of her own – and perhaps share it with someone like Gray. For now, though, she pushed the thought out of her head as she looked over her riding dress.

"I think I should get a new dress for tonight. I'm tired of wearing this riding dress, and since I'm giving you the rest of mine, I should probably find something a little more elegant for dinner," Martha said, looking towards Greta for her input.

"I think that's a grand idea, miss. Families often come to the Honeywell Inn to dine with the travelers. Bill is such a great cook that others come by just for dinner. You could try

Frost's Mercantile to see if they have any ladies' wear in stock, although most ladies either need to sew their own dresses or order them from a catalogue," Greta explained.

Martha sighed, knowing that settling in a small town would have some drawbacks. Her hometown did at least have a lady's boutique, and she wasn't sure what she'd find at a general store that doubled as a depot and restaurant.

"I think I'll go see what Mr. Frost has. Hopefully Mrs. Frost keeps a decent stock," Martha said hopefully.

"Good luck with your shopping," Greta said as she moved towards the door with the bundle of laundry in her hands.

"Greta," Martha called as she watched the woman open the door.

"Yes, miss?"

"I can count on you to keep what you saw a secret, correct?" Martha asked, wondering if she needed to keep the saddlebag on her person.

"Of course, miss!" Greta exclaimed. "No one will hear a word from me, you can count on that."

Martha nodded her head and gave the older woman a smile as the door shut. Alone once again, she took a few deep breaths before crossing the room to the wardrobe and pulling a few bills from the bag. She tucked them into her skirt pocket, and picking up the room key, left the room and locked it tightly behind her. This was the first time anyone had discovered how much money she was travelling with, and she really hoped that she could trust Greta. Saying a quick prayer, she left the inn and headed back to the mercantile.

"How about this one, dear?" Mrs. Frost asked as Martha looked at the small selection of gowns that were currently in stock. She had to admit that Mrs. Frost did have good taste and kept an elegant selection of gowns, as well as gowns for everyday use. But tonight Martha wanted to wear something besides riding clothes or a plain gown. She wanted to dress up for dinner and finally start feeling more herself again. Mrs. Frost held up a green satin dress with pretty lace designs sewn into the hem. "This one will surely enhance your features with that beautiful head of red hair."

Martha chuckled as she took the gown from the woman, a petite lady with long white hair, the kind that looked beautiful with age. Mrs. Frost had it done up in a chignon, which only seemed to make her more charming. "I think you're absolutely right, Mrs. Frost," Martha agreed as she held it over her body, thinking that it would be a close fit to her size. She wouldn't know, though, until she tired it on.

"I think it will be a pretty sweet deal, Sawyer," came the voice of a man. Martha looked down the aisle she was standing at the end of with Mrs. Frost. She saw two young men, both with light brown hair; the one she thought had spoken was taller than the other, while the slightly shorter one had very broad shoulders.

"I don't know, Eddie. I like Sam and all, but you know how Gray is. Aren't you afraid of working for him? And what happens after calving season is over? We will be right back where we are now," the other said as he stopped and looked up at the taller man.

"Sawyer, it's not like there are many job options right now. Josh hired Grant as his full-time deputy for his background and experience, and the local farmers aren't going to need any additional help to harvest this season. We need to learn new skills if we are going to survive," the first man said, his voice soft, although where Martha and Mrs. Frost stood, they could easily hear the whole conversation.

"I'll take the gown, Mrs. Frost," Martha said as she handed it over to the woman.

"Perfect. I'll take it to the front counter and ring it up when you're ready," Mrs. Frost said before she moved away and headed back to the front of the store. Gathering her courage, Martha approached the two young men.

"Excuse me, gentlemen. I don't mean to eavesdrop, but I overheard you speaking about a man named Gray. Are you by chancing speaking of Gray Jenkins, of Slater's Ranch?"

The two stopped talking and turned their gaze towards her, both of them surprised that such a beautiful woman would be coming up to them. They both gave her a goofy smile that made Martha a tad uncomfortable. Perhaps she shouldn't be so friendly to strangers.

"Why, yes, miss. We're talking of Gray Jenkins. Certainly a fine young lady such as yourself wouldn't want anything to do with like a guy like Gray. This is my brother Sawyer, and I'm Eddie Murtaugh," Eddie said as he extended his hand towards her. She simply dipped her head, and Eddie quickly put her hand down.

"I am indeed curious about Mr. Jenkins and would care to understand your opinion," Martha replied, hoping to perhaps learn the true nature of Gray before she met the man. But the way these brothers were looking at her gave her the idea that perhaps she'd made a wrong choice there.

She could practically feel Sawyer undressing her with his eyes.

"Well, I can say that many women are curious about Gray but never seem to stick with him very long, if you now what I mean. He's not the long-term relationship type, which is why he's an old, lonely man now. I'm sure I could give you more to be curious about," Eddie said as he winked at her.

Martha refrained from rolling her eyes as she turned to leave. When she felt a hand on her arm, she lashed out and slapped her assailant. She turned to see Eddie's surprised face as he held his hand up to where she'd slapped him. Sawyer gave her a quizzical look as he stared at her.

"Please, don't ever touch me again," Martha stuttered, and she left in a worry, paying Mrs. Frost for her dress without another word, and then making haste back to the inn.

Martha didn't stop to say hello to Bill at the front counter and practically ran up the stairs to her room, taking so long to unlock her door that she almost threw the key to the floor in frustration. Closing her eyes and taking a steadying breath, she finally unlocked the door and stepped inside, closing the door and locking it again before pocketing the key. She felt like crumbling to the ground, but made it to the bed where she laid out her new gown, and then slumped down into one of the chairs.

She took several minutes to steady her breathing as she thought about how she had reacted in the store. It was so natural to strike out that it frightened her to think she had acted so coldly. Surely if she had just told Eddie to remove his hand he would have done so, but she hadn't even thought about that. All she had thought was that she needed to escape the situation as quickly as possible.

"Get a hold of yourself, Martha," she chastised, knowing that she needed to bring her nerves under control. Deciding it would do her some good to take a nice long, hot bath before dinner, she rose and made her way back downstairs to order up the tub.

CHAPTER 10

*G*ray pulled his horse back into a trot as he neared town. It had been a while since he'd made the trip, usually only coming in seeking a warm body for the night or a good time at Handy's, the local saloon. This time he was heading to the inn with hopes of meeting the woman he'd exchanged letters with. Gray wasn't yet sure how to feel about the idea of Mary, or what he'd learn about the woman once they met in person. Could she have lied about who she was? Perhaps this Mary wasn't even the one he'd been corresponding with, and the whole thing would be a huge misunderstanding.

Gray tried to get his emotions under control as he neared the inn, dismounted, and tied the reins to the hitching post out front. He could hear plenty of voices coming from inside as dinner seemed to be underway. Taking a deep breath, he put on his mask of emotions and went in.

Strolling in, Gray smiled as he neared the front counter,

spotting Greta manning the counter. "Good evening, beautiful. How is my favorite widow this evening?" he asked.

"Oh, Gray, you charmer. What brings you to the inn tonight? Meeting some lady or another?" Greta said with a knowing smile.

"I'm sure hoping to, Mrs. Royal. I hear there's a young lady named Mary staying at the inn and might be dining in tonight?" Gray questioned, hoping Greta could either confirm or deny what Sam had told him.

Greta stilled as she thought of Mary, that young girl who looked so innocent and not Gray's usual type. Everyone knew that Gray was a womanizer and often older, lonely women flocked to him. She wasn't sure what intentions Gray had with the young woman she had met earlier. Feeling protective of the girl, Greta narrowed her eyes at Gray.

"And what would a bad guy like you want of a good girl like Mary?" Greta asked as she folded her arms over her bosom.

Gray smiled his charming smile as he leaned over the counter towards her. "It might be hard to believe, my dear, but Mary and I have been writing letters to each other. Mary is my mail-order bride," he said in a low voice, not wanting anyone to overhear them. Greta was clearly surprised, as she playfully slapped Gray's arm.

"Why would a man like you be interested in marriage? Not like that thought ever crossed your mind before," she replied, not believe a word he had just spoken.

"Well, you see, Mrs. Royal, you of all people would understand that there comes a time in one's life when you just don't want to be lonely anymore. And all the great women I've crossed paths with in the past weren't exactly looking for a husband, if you know what I mean," Gray said, his mask seeming to fall away as he spoke honestly with the older woman.

Greta softened as she reached out her hand and laid it on Gray's, sympathetically. She'd give anything to have Mr. Royal back in her life again, and couldn't imagine going through life having never met or married him.

"She's already seated in the dining room," she said as she pointed towards the room. "I think she could use some company as well, Gray. She didn't look to happy this evening, not like earlier."

"I'll see what I can do, Mrs. Royal. Thank you," Gray said with a tip of his cowboy hat. He straightened, then and moved towards the dining room, looking over the crowd of people.

MARTHA WAS FOCUSING on her dinner of pork roast and green beans, not really paying anyone much attention because she wanted to be more cautious around strangers. She'd let her guard down earlier, having been overly excited about the idea of settling down, and felt that had probably led her to be the person whom the town was gossiping about this evening. Martha could hear those around her whispering intently, when someone sat in the seat across the table from her, drawing her attention.

She gasped as her bright blue eyes met dark onyx. The man before her had very broad shoulders and probably stood taller than her, should he be standing up. But he was staring at her from across the table they now shared. After noticing the slight greying of his hair around the temples, and the dimple in his check when he smiled at her, obviously enjoying her reaction, Martha had a pretty good idea who was sitting across from her.

"It seems the saying is true," she started with, reaching forward to gather her water and take a long drink.

"And what saying would that be, my dear?" Gray asked as he leaned forward, having loved the surprised look on Mary's face.

"Speak of the devil and he shall appear," Martha said with a smirk, meeting the man's eyes once more. Gray let out a laugh, a pleasant sound that Martha thought she might never tire of hearing.

"So, you've been talking about me all day, and you think I'm a devil," Gray said, his smile charming and alluring. Martha couldn't stop staring at him, his handsome features not what she was expecting from a man over a decade older than her. She was pleasantly surprised, indeed.

"I might have spoken with a few about you, indirectly. And I don't know if I should consider you the devil or not. You sure have the charm of one. Now I'm curious to see if you have the heart of one," Martha replied before she'd truly thought about what she was saying. Gray noticed the way she seemed to reflect on something; the way a streak of sadness ran through her eyes as she momentarily looked away. And when Mary turned her gaze back on him, she smiled brightly, as if trying to cover up some sort of emotion.

"Well, Miss Carver, I can assure you I'm a perfect gentleman and would never treat a woman poorly or force her to do something she doesn't want," Gray said, lowering his voice and speaking with complete honesty.

Martha could tell his words were sincere, and she wondered just how much she might have given away through her poor choice of words. It seemed that even when she was trying to flirt she couldn't completely get rid of her pain, or her past.

"Well, Mr. Jenkins, I'm sure you'll prove that in time," Martha replied as she held her hand out to him. "It's a pleasure to have finally made your acquaintance."

Gray took her hand firmly in his and placed his lips to her knuckles, taking his time with the kiss as his eyes locked with hers. Martha felt a spark race through her from where Gray had placed his lips on her skin, filling her with warmth all over. She withdrew her hand then, trying not to appear as startled as she felt. She'd never had that kind of reaction from any sort of kiss before.

"Please, Mary, call me Gray. After all, we've already decided not to be so formal," Gray said, reminding her of their letters.

"Of course, Gray. Have you eaten?" Martha asked, not wanting to appear rude by eating in front of his man.

"I have not, but please don't wait on me. I'll order once the server comes around," Gray said, pleased to see that Mary wasn't someone to be shy around food. "What you have looks delicious."

"It is," Martha confirmed as she took another bite. It would be best for Gray to understand just what type of woman she was: not someone to wait around to eat just because it was considered ladylike. Between bites, Martha took the time to ask, "Did you happen to receive my last letter?"

Gray watched her, noting her full lips and thinking how much he'd enjoy kissing them. Her question brought his eyes back to hers. "I did not. No, it was Sam who told me he suspected you were in town. Sam heard from Sheriff Ryder that a mysterious woman with fiery red hair had rode into town."

Martha couldn't help but smile at the description of herself, and also at the fact that some small-town characteristics were the same no matter where she travelled. "I'm guessing Spruce Valley doesn't get many visitors," she said as she pushed aside her finished plate just in time for dinner to arrive at the table for Gray.

"You're correct in thinking such. But it's also not every day that an unknown young woman rides into town by herself," Gray confirmed before taking a bite. He enjoyed the savory taste of the pork roast, pleased to find the pork still juicy and not dried out. He noted that the rub used to season the pork was excellent and decided that he'd have to ask Bill what his recipe was. Bringing his attention back to Mary, he saw her watching him carefully.

"Well, needless to say, I'm not like most women," was all Martha was willing to say at this time. This was neither the time nor the place to be speaking freely of her past.

"I'm sure that's one of the many things I'm going to like about you," Gray said encouragingly between bites. Mary smiled, and Gray thought her eyes became even brighter. He'd never thought that placing an ad in the *Matrimonial Times* would bring someone as beautiful as Mary to him. Now he just hoped he could keep her and actually start a meaningful relationship with a woman. Surely he could start fresh with her.

Hearing the British accent in his voice, Martha asked, "So, what brought you to America from England?" She watched as his eyes softened, as though in memory.

"Well, as you can imagine, living in England and travelling out West are completely different experiences. I was tired of the same boring life every day, and, wanting to pave my own way in life instead of having to live the life given to me, I left everything in England behind and came to America intent on using my hands to make my fortune," Gray explained.

Martha couldn't help but laugh as she shook her head. "That's a whole lot of words to explain absolutely nothing," she said.

Gray winked at her as he finished eating. "As you can imagine, my dear, there is something in my past I was running from, but I don't care to discuss it over dinner," he explained. Martha nodded her head, agreeing fully. "Now, since we are both done, would you care to join me for a stroll? The night air isn't too chilly."

Martha raised an eyebrow at Gray, a smirk on her lips, as she considered the offer. A spark of energy went through Gray as she gave him that look. He found her positively divine as she wondered whether or not to join him on a night walk. They had only just met and had exchanged very few letters, so he understood her hesitance. But she looked so lovely in her emerald gown that he wanted an excuse to continue enjoying some time with her, away from prying eyes.

"I'd love to accompany you, Gray. I could certainly use

some fresh air," Martha finally agreed, rising with him after he set a few bills on the table. "Thank you," she said as she took the arm he offered her.

"The pleasure is all mine, Mary. After all, I can only imagine the financial burden you've been under after travelling for so long," he said as he led her from the dining room and out of the front of the inn. Martha felt like she could breath easier once they were a few yards away from the inn. And though the air was a bit chilly that evening, Martha hardly noticed because she felt so warm being so close to Gray.

"Before I left Wisconsin, I sold my family's land, never planning on returning again. I had a decent amount from when my father passed away, and I also sold the cattle, not intending on keeping the family business. I worked as a waitress and made a decent wage. So, all in all, I have plenty to get by on. Granted, it won't last forever, so I hope to find some sort of employment before to long," Martha explained, not wanting to share the bit about the stolen money she had hidden away in her room at the inn. Tonight was not the night for those types of details.

"Well, Mary, I'm not sure what you're hoping to do, but Spruce Valley isn't a large place," Gray said, trying to think if he knew of any open positions.

"I'm not too worried about it right now," Martha confessed as she walked close to him. "I hope to become more acquainted with Spruce Valley and the people here, and hopefully find my own place to stay."

The more time Gray spent with Mary, the more curious he became. Since she was more concerned with a place to stay than with employment, he wondered just how well-off she was. They walked in silence for a while as they wound through the town. Martha noticed several empty stores and wondered what types of business Spruce Valley could benefit from. *She* could certainly use a women's boutique, and having a local bank would make things more convenient for her, instead of keeping her money in a saddlebag.

"Well, I'll be busy for a while since we're right in the middle of calving season, but once things die down a bit at the ranch I'd love to help you get settled. Sam and Josh know practically everything that's going on in this town, besides Mayor Delphine herself, so I'm sure we can help you find a place," Gray said, smiling down at Mary. She returned his smile as they made their way back to the inn. Gray found himself not wanting the night to end. He couldn't remember the last time he had enjoyed the company of a woman without the intention of spending the night together. He realized this kind of company was something he'd been missing out on for a long time, and he didn't want to let Mary go.

"I appreciate your kindness, Gray. Most people here seem to be quite friendly," Martha said; but then she thought about Eddie and Sawyer.

Gray noticed the way her brows furrowed, and couldn't help but ask, "Has anyone not been friendly to you since you got into town?"

"I wouldn't say unkind, really," Martha said as she stood outside the inn, her arm still resting on Gray's. "But the Murtaugh brothers were a bit forward when I ran into them today at Frost's Mercantile. Mrs. Frost helped me pick out this beautiful gown and I overheard them talking about coming to work for you on the ranch. When I heard your name, I inquired of you, but they seemed more interested in knowing why I'd asked than answering my simple question about their opinion of you. And since you might hear it from someone else, I'll just come out and tell you: when Eddie stopped me from leaving, probably to flirt with me, I slapped him. To be honest, I think it startled both of us. It was just a reflex, to tell the truth. But I'm sure I hurt his feelings."

Gray suppressed a laugh at the thought of Mary slapping Eddie, but he could tell that she was embarrassed by the whole thing by the way she spoke quickly and averted her eyes from him. He squeezed her hand, drawing her attention back to him. Martha noted the dimple in his cheek and the way his eyes swam with humor, causing her to smile in return. "I would have paid to see you give one of the Murtaugh brothers a good whooping. I'm sure Eddie deserved it," Gray said.

Martha just shrugged her shoulders as she finally let go of Gray and neared the front door, knowing she should go inside and settle down for the night. But he caught her hand and drew her back to him. Even though he knew he was being forward, he didn't want to miss the opportunity to leave a good impression on Mary. And as she looked up into his eyes, Martha wondered if he was going to kiss her. This was the part she had been dreading when it came to the idea of being courted by a man.

Noting the fear in her eyes, Gray dropped her hand. "I hope you have a pleasant evening, Mary. If things go well, I'll visit you again tomorrow evening. With the Murtaugh brothers coming to work with us in the morning, I'm sure I could get away for a bit," he said, instead of wrapping his arms around her and planting a soft kiss on her lips. No: Mary would have to be won over with words tonight instead of his normal charms.

"I'd like that, Gray. I hope you have a good night as well," Martha replied. She tried to give him a genuine smile, but Gray could tell it was contrived, by the way it didn't reach her eyes. She turned away from him then and went inside the inn, not stopping to chat with Greta as she ascended the stairs and went to her room.

Gray stood for a few minutes before he turned away from the inn and went over to his horse, his mind deep in thought. He had enjoyed his evening with Mary, finding her both humorous and charming, and he was pleasantly surprised by her beauty. But he could tell that she was hiding something. Still, he would give her all the time she needed to open up to him, especially if she was willing to give a man like him a chance of a happy, married life.

CHAPTER 11

The next morning, after enjoying a light breakfast in her room, Martha thought of her evening with Gray. She was surprised how handsome he was, and by his gentlemanly character. She had loved to listen to his British accent and had thoroughly enjoyed the feeling of him next to her as they had walked through town together. When the idea of love crossed her mind, though, she dashed her thoughts to pieces, knowing she'd never allow herself to become that vulnerable with a man again.

Instead, Martha turned her thoughts to the task at hand. She wanted to go out and see if she could learn anything from anyone about a possible apartment or house to rent. Having dressed in one of the freshly laundered gowns Greta had delivered to her that morning, she pinned back her long auburn hair, allowing it to flow down her back for the most part. She felt refreshed and ready to take on the day as she left her room, locked the door behind her, and headed out of the inn.

"GOOD MORNING, BOYS!" Gray called as he stepped down from the front porch of the ranch house, having enjoyed an early breakfast with the Slaters. Tom had just come in from the pasture and had gone straight to bed, and Jensen was still in bed, so Gray had enjoyed hearing about Sam's experience in the pasture last night, and also the way Lucy had laughed when she gave details of Sam's panicked reaction to a cow giving birth. They had spent the morning laughing while Sam simply scowled at his best friend and wife. Now Gray met the Murtaugh brothers out front as they arrived at the ranch.

"Morning, Mr. Jenkins," Eddie said he approached the intimidating man with Sawyer. He sure didn't like the cold stare Gray gave them, but Eddie wasn't going to pass up an opportunity for employment, and he knew that Dr. Slater was one of the wealthiest men in town.

"I hope you two are ready for a full day's work," Gray said, pointedly looking at Eddie. The young man didn't like the way the older man was looking at him, and prayed he wasn't in over his head when it came to trying his luck at ranch work.

"Yes, sir." Sawyer responded for Eddie, giving his brother a strange look. He wasn't sure how Eddie had gotten on Gray's bad side, but he could tell something was up by the way Gray was staring at his brother.

"Well, then. Saddle up and let's get to it. We need to get the herd moved to the far pasture and separate the expecting cows from the rest. I expect full cooperation today, fellas. You have to be fully focused and ready to follow my commands at a moment's notice," Gray said sternly, fixing his gaze on Eddie, who seemed to visibly slink back from his stare. "And if I ever hear of you laying a hand on Mary Carver again, she won't be the only one slapping you in the face."

Eddie's eyes grew wide and Sawyer let out a snicker. Gray ignored them as he saddled his horse and made his way to the pasture gate, the brothers quick to mount their own horses and follow. "Guess you insulted the boss man's girl," Sawyer whispered to his brother as they passed through the gate, but Eddie didn't respond and only scolded his brother, his gut telling him that Gray was going to work him hard for nothing more than flirting with a young lady. How was he supposed to know that Gray could be interested in a woman for more than just a warm body to hold at night? Things were certainly going to be interesting for Sawyer and himself.

AFTER STOPPING in at all the local businesses and introducing herself, Martha felt strangely fatigued, though she didn't think she'd done that much, and decided to stop at the Eatery for a something small to eat and a cup of tea. She'd met Zachariah Welliver, the furniture maker, the Reverend Paul Gibbons and his wife, Annette, at the church, Grant Carlson, the Sheriff's deputy on his rounds around town, and Jenny Crawford, the local schoolteacher on her way to the schoolhouse. It had been a wild morning visiting and talking with so many people, and though they had all been quite friendly, Martha still hadn't heard of any leads about places she could rent right away. She was starting to feel a little hopeless as she went into Frost's

Mercantile and headed to the back of the store to find an empty table to sit at.

"Hello, Mary. How are you doing today?" Nell asked as the older woman can around to her table.

Martha smiled at her as she took a deep breath. "I am doing okay, Nell. I've been trying to meet as many people as I can this morning, trying to find someone who might know of a place I could rent," she explained as she accepted a menu from Nell, not really intending on using it.

"Oh, that must be exciting. It sounds like you plan on staying a while, then," Nell said with a smile.

"I do hope to make Spruce Valley my new home. I'm just hoping there will be opportunities here to make it worth it," Martha confessed as she set down the menu. "I'll just have a cup of the wonderful tea you make, and whatever small snack you'd suggest."

This made Nell smile even more. "Certainly, my dear," she said as she headed off towards the kitchen.

"Excuse me, miss. I couldn't help but overhear you talking about opportunities here in town," an older woman said from two tables over. Martha looked towards the voice and watched as the plump woman, who looked to be seventy-ish, approached her and took a seat at her table. "Mrs. Delphine Stavros."

Martha shook the woman's hand. "Mary Carver, pleased to meet you. If I've heard correctly, you're Spruce Valley's Mayor."

Mrs. Stavros smiled widely as she nodded. Her dark brown hair was pulled back into a bun, and though she smiled, she had a sense of authority around her. "That would be true. My husband, Anton, was Mayor for several years, and when he died I took the position over since no one else wanted it. I like to think that I'm serving in my husband's memory as he would have done for this fine town," Mrs. Stavros explained with a pleasant smile.

"That's very noble of you," Martha replied as she eyed the woman. "And yes, you overheard correctly. I'm looking for new opportunities here in Spruce Valley. I just arrived yesterday and hope to get settled as quickly as I can."

Mrs. Stavros raised an eyebrow at Martha, a small smirk on her lips. "And what brings such a beautiful young lady as yourself to this fine town?" she asked.

"Well, I've been corresponding with Mr. Jenkins, and after meeting him last night for dinner I plan to stick around and see where things lead. Besides, I have nowhere else to go and Spruce Valley looks like as good a place as any to settle down and grow roots," Martha explained, having a feeling it was easier to come straight out with the truth with the Mayor instead of beating around the bush. Mrs. Stavros didn't look like the type of woman who liked to be led around.

Mrs. Stavros considered the young girl's words for a moment, as Nell returned with a pot of tea for the both of them and a small plate of sugar cookies. The women thanked her as she left, then turned their attention back to each other.

"Mr. Jenkins is a lucky man to have attracted such a beautiful young lady. I didn't know he was the marrying type," Mrs. Stavros said as she tried to think whether she had ever seen Gray in a serious relationship.

"Gray has been quite honest with me about his past, and his genuine sincerity is what makes me think that he could be a worthy husband," Martha said pointedly, hoping this woman hadn't come over to cause her any trouble. Since Gray was known as a womanizer, it wasn't unlikely that she would come across someone who would oppose the idea of Gray ever being a worthy husband.

"I agree that Gray has always been a gentleman whenever we've met in social situations. I'm Dr. Slater's neighbor, so I've run into the ranch hand from time to time. And since we are the only two Brits in the area, it's nice to visit with a fellow countryman," Mrs. Stavros explained as she took a sip of her tea, enjoying as always the fine tea Nell made. She could tell that Martha enjoyed it too, by the way she smiled after she took a sip.

"I'm glad to hear your good opinion of the man, considering you are the Mayor," Martha replied. She was starting to see just how small Spruce Valley really was. Only two days in town and she'd already met some of the most important people there were to meet.

"Indeed. And I think anyone would be lucky to catch Gray's eye. He's always been a charmer, but deep down he's as manly as the rest of them: in need of someone to love and to have someone love him in return," Mrs. Stavros said with a far-off look in her eyes. Martha could only imagine she was thinking of her late husband. Mrs. Stavros then refocused her eyes on her. "So, what kind of opportunities are you looking for besides finding a husband?"

Martha smiled as she set aside her teacup. "Well, I'm wanting to find a place to stay that isn't the inn. Though Mr. Eckert is a nice host and Mrs. Royal is the kindest housekeeper I've ever met, I look forward to having a space of my own. Besides that, I will want of some sort of employment before too long. I have means, but they won't last forever," Martha explained, figuring the best person to talk to about these matters had to be the Mayor.

Mrs. Stavros nodded her head in understanding as she thought about current possibilities for the young lady. "I see. Well, there aren't any vacant houses at the moment. Spruce Valley is mainly made up of farmers and ranchers outside of town, and those who live in town have built their own houses and businesses to sustain themselves. In the past, my husband had other buildings put up, in hopes of new businesses coming to town, but it just hasn't happened yet. I would suggest considering having your own home built," Mrs. Stavros explained.

Martha felt dejected at the idea, for she was hoping to move into a place sooner than later. She didn't want to wait months for a home to be built and have to continue living at the inn. That would force her to spend all her money faster than she'd intended to.

"Of course," Mrs. Stavros continued, "if you and Gray do decide to marry, I'm sure you'll want to build a house together."

Martha pondered this, never having thought of the possibility before. "I guess you're right, Madam Mayor," she replied as she took another sip of tea.

"Please, dear, call me Delphine. "Madam Mayor" sounds like a pompous title. I'm human, after all," Mrs. Stavros said with a contagious smile.

"Delphine it is. Well, I guess I can wait to see how things go between Gray and myself. Till then, I'm sure Mr. Eckert won't mind me staying for a bit longer than I'd intended," Martha settled with, wondering what else she was going to do with her time if she wasn't out looking for a place to stay. She knew that Gray would be working hard at the ranch and wouldn't be in town till that evening.

"You seem to be a woman of action, someone who likes to be moving and doing," Mrs. Stavros observed as she watched Martha look around in the room as though deep in thought.

Martha smiled as she nodded her head. "Indeed. I've been travelling these past four weeks since I sold my family's ranch and decided to relocate. After all, with no family there was nothing keeping me in Wisconsin. But with nowhere to go and nothing to do, I feel a bit restless," Martha explained.

Mrs. Stavros was surprised to hear more about Mary's past, but she wasn't going to pressure the young woman to tell her more. She knew what it was like to want to move on after the death of a love one, and if it hadn't been for the vacant Mayor's position, Mrs. Stavros wouldn't have known what do to with herself. Her daughter Elena was a delight to visit with, especially given that Mrs. Stavros had four grandchildren to play with during her visits, but everyone wants a purpose in life that gives it meaning. For Delphine, that purpose had been helping to run the town in her husband's name.

"What would you think of accompanying me to Dr. Slater's ranch? I've been meaning to pay Mrs. Slater a visit, since she is expecting and I care to know how she is faring these days," Mrs. Stavros offered, knowing that any young lady being courted by a man would take any opportunity to see her beau as often as she could. That, and it would also give her the opportunity to see where Gray spent most of his time and the people he spent his time with.

"That's very kind of you, Delphine. I'd love a chance to see the ranch and continue meeting the locals. Having come from a small town myself, I know how important it is to meet everyone and make acquaintances," Martha said, happy that this new opportunity had arisen. She didn't want to appear like she was spying on Gray, but she couldn't deny that it would be pleasant to see him sooner than planned.

"I'm sure Lucy would love to meet you, too. With her being so far along, she doesn't make it into town as often as she did, and I'm sure she could use the company," Mrs. Stavros said.

The two finished their tea and cookies, and soon headed out of the Eatery together, Mrs. Stavros leading Martha to her buggy in front of the mercantile. Together the pair headed out of town, Mrs. Stavros filling Martha in on everything she knew about the place: how it first started many years ago, and little titbits about all the townspeople. Martha was certain that she was going to enjoy hearing all she could from Delphine, and as they continued on their way, her pulse started to race at the prospect of seeing Gray in action on the ranch.

CHAPTER 12

*W*hen Mrs. Stavros announced that they were pulling down the lane to Dr. Slater's ranch, Martha craned her neck this way and that to see everything she could. A small, one-storey, white clapboard ranch house stood a little way down the lane on the right. A large red barn had been erected farther down the lane, with wooden fencing running out from the back of it. Several horses grazed in the pasture, and she could make out the shape of cattle in the distance. The sight made her feel like she was coming home, as she remembered similar details of her life growing up while her father raised a small herd of cattle. So many sights and smells reminded her of her childhood and her father, bringing tears to her eyes. But she pushed it all away as she continued to look around.

A sea of prairie grass stretched away as far as Martha could see, meeting the dazzling blue sky above the horizon. Maple and birch trees dotted the ranch, and there was a white bunkhouse on the left of the driveway. She assumed this building was where all the ranch hands lived, including Gray. And with it being the middle of the day, she assumed Gray would be out in the pasture. So she was pleasantly surprised to see him stepping down from the front porch of the ranch house with a small group of men. But her heart thudded in her chest when she noticed the Murtaugh brothers.

As Mrs. Stavros brought the buggy around to the front driveway it drew the attention of everyone out front. Martha looked over at Gray and smiled, their eyes locking as he smiled in return, placing his hands on his hips. The stance filled Martha with warmth, as it did to see a man looking at her like that. She'd never felt like this before.

"Why you two just gawking? Help those ladies down from the buggy!" Gray barked, directing his attention towards Eddie and Sawyer. The two brothers jumped into action, Eddie running around the buggy to help Mrs. Stavros down before taking the reins, while Sawyer helped Martha alight from the vehicle. As the women approached the porch, the brothers made quick work of leading the buggy to the barn to settle the horse.

"My, my, Mr. Jenkins, I do believe I've never seen those two move as quickly as I just witnessed," Mrs. Stavros commented as she looked back over her shoulder at the barn.

"Let's just say that I've put the fear of God in them,' Gray said.

Mrs. Stavros then went into the house, leaving Gray alone with Martha.

'I have ensured that Eddie will not be bothering you again, Mary," Gray said as he took a step closer to her.

Martha blushed as she looked up into his onyx eyes. "Why, thank you, Gray. It always makes a lady feel nice to know there's a man out there willing to protect her."

Gray winked at her. "Well, you have a man right here willing to do just that for you."

This only made Martha blush even more as she looked up into Gray's charming face. She never imagined she'd feel this way around a man again, but there was something in the way Gray looked at her, all mixed in with his sincere words, that almost had her believing she could honestly trust him. But then she remembered what had happened to her the last time she'd trusted a man, and her silly feelings quickly left her.

"I thank you again, Gray. If you'll excuse me, I told Mrs. Stavros I'd meet Mrs. Slater and visit with them for a bit," Martha said quickly, and dipped her head before heading into the ranch house.

Gray sighed as he watched her go, not moving till the door was closed in front of him. It frustrated him to see how quickly Mary had shut him down, but he couldn't fault her. It was obvious to him that something was haunting the young lady, and he was going to give her time to not only get used to him and a new town, but also to the idea of opening up to him.

He stepped off the porch and made quick haste to catch up to the Murtaugh brothers, enjoying putting those two through their paces as they learned what it meant to be a ranch hand.

"IT'S SUCH a pleasure to finally make yer acquaintance, Miss Carver. Gray's been teasing us with small details of ya from yer letters, so I can't tell ya what a relief it is to finally meet ya," Mrs. Slater said, her Irish brogue obvious to Martha. From looks alone – she had long black hair and blue eyes – she didn't look very Irish, but her words made it quite obvious.

"You're too kind, Mrs. Slater. Thank you for welcoming me when you weren't expecting Mrs. Stavros to be bringing along a visitor. You have such a lovely home," Martha commented, more curious to know what exactly Gray had said about her to his employers. They sat in the parlor, Martha in a wing-back chair close to the fireplace. This made Lucy smile because she knew that it was the seat that Gray took to every evening to give his daily report to Sam.

"Bein' so far from town, I do love receiving visitors. And since I'm so far 'long, it makes it hard to travel into town. So this is quite a pleasant surprise. Ye are most welcome any time you fancy a trip to the ranch," Lucy said as she poured tea and handed the Mayor and Martha a cup.

"Thank you, Lucy. I do appreciate the tea. How have you been faring lately?" Mrs. Stavros asked. As the two ladies chatted about Mrs. Slater's condition, Lucy describing the uncomfortable aspects of pregnancy (though she was quite joyful to be expecting), Martha looked around the house. It was finely furnished, and she could surmise that the Slaters were well off. As she thought of the house she'd like one day, Martha reasoned that she'd have Mrs. Slater help her with the decorating since her house was so nicely done.

"So, Miss Carver," Mrs. Slater said, drawing Martha's attention back to the conversation, "what do you think of Spruce Valley so far?"

Martha smiled as she set down her cup. "To be honest, it reminds me a bit of home. I come from a small town in Wisconsin and I've missed the small-community feel of home. I've only been in town for two days but feel I've met some wonderful families. I know how important community is in a small town, so I want to meet everyone I can," Martha explained, causing everyone to chuckle. They all understood the importance of this in a close community.

"Granted," Martha continued, "the only down side is how quick word spreads in town. Why, I just arrived yesterday and already I've been able to meet Gray without having to say hardly a word."

Another round of laughter ensued before Mrs. Slater said, "I do have to agree with that, Miss Carver. My dear Sam was just full of enthusiasm as he talked about bumping into the Sheriff at lunch and learning about yer arrival from Josh. Sam just couldn't wait to tell Gray. Some things ye just can't avoid in a small town."

Mrs. Stavros nodded her head and mentioned, "I met Miss Carver at the Eatery today. I overheard her and Nell talking about opportunities in town."

Mrs. Slater sighed as she turned her gaze back to Martha. "That has been a wee bit of a problem, hasn't it? There doesn't seem to be enough jobs to go around. I was hoping I could start my boutique before to long," she said with another long sigh.

"Are you hopeful of opening up a women's boutique?" Martha asked, thinking it would be a wonderful idea.

"Aye, Miss Carver. My family is from Buffalo, New York, and there are some things I miss about home and living in a big city. I've always had an interest in fashion, and I still have plenty of family back in New York who keep me updated on the latest. I'd want to bring the latest to Spruce Valley and give women the opportunity to have dresses for nice occasions, and more durable, fashionable fabrics for everyday gowns," Mrs. Slater explained. The way the woman was smiling told Martha just how passionate she was about the idea. "But alas, I don't have the ability to go into town and make things happen now."

An idea sparked inside of Martha, and as a woman of action she was ready to begin then and there. "Mrs. Slater, I think Spruce Valley could absolutely use a women's boutique. And with your connections in New York, plus your experience, I think you'd make a wonderful businesswoman. I'd love to help you bring this idea to reality, seeing as I need employment of my own; quite frankly I like to have something to keep myself busy with. I have my own horse and can come out to the ranch to run the business side with you, and then manage the store in town till your little one comes along and you feel up to coming into town yourself," she said, her excitement showing in her voice.

Lucy's blue eyes grew huge as a large smile crossed her face. "Ye'd really do that for me? I mean, I'm not sure what I'd be able to pay ya right away, there would be all sorts of things to figure out," Mrs. Slater said as she pushed back her hair, trying to keep her composure even though she was rather excited about the idea of someone helping her make her dream come true. With her dear husband at work each day, she really didn't have someone to talk to about her fashion ideas, and having another woman to work with would be fantastic.

"I'm not to worried about pay right now, Mrs. Slater. I

would be happy just to help you get set up and we can worry about those details later," Martha said, her mind already racing to remember the various empty store fronts she'd seen earlier in town. She wondered which one would be best for the boutique.

"Please, Miss Carver, call me Lucy. After all, it seems we'll be more than just acquaintances soon 'nough," Mrs. Slater said with a wink.

"Thank you, Lucy," Martha replied, feeling a bit guilty about giving her false name to so many good people. But she knew it was for her own safety, and instead of thinking about her past Martha turned her thoughts to the future as the three women started talking about the boutique and the business side of things.

After a while, Mrs. Stavros stood and announced, "I really must be getting home, my dears. It's been a lovely visit. Miss Carver, I presume you can make your way back to town on your own?"

"Absolutely, Mrs. Stavros. I'll make sure Mary gets back this evening. Or I should say that Gray will ensure Mary's safe return," Lucy said with a chuckle.

"Then I leave her in your capable hands, Lucy. Till next time," Mrs. Stavros said as she made her departure. Martha couldn't help but blush, but quickly turned the conversation back to the boutique, pleased to be having such a wonderful project to work on, and also a good excuse to stay longer in the hopes of visiting with Gray soon enough.

CHAPTER 13

*G*ray was beat by the time the sun was setting over the ranch. He road in alone from the pasture, having already dismissed Eddie and Sawyer for the day. Though those two had experience working as deputies – and causing a bit of trouble themselves in town with the young ladies – the Murtaugh brothers were nonetheless hard workers. And even though they were green ranch hands, they proved to learn real quick and be fast to follow orders. Gray could actually endure calving season knowing he had two fresh hands to work with.

He led his horse into the barn and then worked on taking off her saddle and brushing her down. Jensen came in. He had a rather large smile on his old face, as though he was waiting to tell Gray something pretty amazing.

"Have out with it, old man. I don't have time to dawdle," Gray said as Jensen continued to watch him, his arms crossed, with that smile on his face.

"Oh, it's nothing, really. But the misses has had such fine company today – a young lady with beautiful fiery red hair," Jensen said teasingly, giving Gray a wink when the man turned towards him, closing his horse's stall behind him.

"I'm glad to hear that Lucy and Mary have been keeping each other company. I didn't expect her to have stayed so long when I ran into her after lunch," Gray said with a smirk as he saw Jensen's face relax into a scowl. Gray couldn't help but laugh as he said, "Sorry to ruin the surprise."

Jensen shook his head and threw up his arms as he left the barn. Gray followed after him to the bunkhouse, intent on cleaning up before heading to the ranch house. He didn't want to smell like cattle while trying to impress Mary.

As Gray was washing in the water closet, he heard Jensen say, "It's sure getting crowded around her with all these young people movin' about."

Gray stuck his head out and said, "Don't you worry, old man. There will always be room for you here."

As Gray finished cleaning his face and arms, he heard Jensen take a long sigh. He stopped what he was doing then and walked over to where Jensen was sitting, in what was the common area of the bunkhouse; just sitting, with his arms crossed and his eyes towards the fireplace that kept the building warm in the winter.

"What's bothering you, old man?" Gray asked as he sat down in a chair next to Jensen.

It took the older man a few seconds before he opened his mouth. "Seeing the Murtaugh boys on the ranch makes me worried that I won't be needed here any longer," he said softly, not moving his eyes from the fireplace. Gray nodded his head, understanding the man's point of view.

"Jensen, there is one thing I can guarantee you, no matter who comes and goes on this ranch: you, my good sir, will always have a place here. I know the Slaters don't say it, but you're like family to them, to all of us. Hell, I bet you'd make a fine grandpa once Lucy's baby comes along," Gray said, a twinkle in his eyes at the thought of Jensen playing with a baby.

Jensen's eyebrows rose at the thought of that, as he finally looked over at Gray. "Ya really think so?" he said softly, never having really thought about it before.

"Absolutely, my dear fellow," Gray said as he slapped Jensen's back good-naturedly. "You belong here just as much as those cattle out in the field do. And even when the day comes that you don't have the strength to pull yourself up into a saddle anymore, the Slaters are still going to want her hear."

Gray enjoyed the way the old man nodded his head, a smile on his face once more. With that, he left the man to his thoughts and went to change into some fresh clothes.

"MISS CARVER, it's been a pleasure to have you in our home this evening. I can't tell you the last time I saw my dear Lucy this excited," Dr. Slater said as Martha and Lucy sat at the dining table with him. They were enjoying a cup of coffee after the dinner Martha and Lucy had prepared for the ranch hands. Martha was a little disappointed that Gray hadn't come in from the pasture yet, but Dr. Slater had assured her that she could stay till they had visited with Gray. Martha felt like it was a lifetime ago since she'd ridden out with Mrs. Stavros to visit with Lucy. She had no idea that she'd enter into a business with the woman. But after spending the afternoon with her, she was so excited at the idea of opening a boutique that she hadn't wanted to leave.

"The pleasure is all mine, Dr. Slater. I would have never thought that coming to Spruce Valley would bring such a good hand of fate," Martha replied as she set her coffee cup aside. She felt pleasantly comfortable after helping Lucy prepare a large meal for everyone. She wasn't used to cooking for so many people and found the experience educational. Lucy had spent part of the afternoon talking about what it had been like coming to Spruce Valley herself as a mail-order bride and having to learn so much about living in the frontier. Martha could understand the woman's plight, if you weren't used to rising early and making most of what you needed. She also had suppressed a laugh when Lucy explained how she had to learn to ride a horse and drive a buggy from Greta. Martha would have loved to see that.

"Please, call me Sam. I only allow patients to call me Dr. Slater anyways," Sam said as he took a long drink from his coffee.

"Very well, then," Martha replied.

"Mary, where do ye plan to stay while yer in town? I know that the Honeywell Inn is pleasant enough, but it's not a long-term solution," Lucy said, another thought coming to mind as she remembered how stuffy her room had been while she was staying there. It also held several bad memories, so she couldn't really imagine Mary being there for any longer than was needed.

"Well, that's what I started my day off doing. I visited with anyone I came across in hopes of meeting more people from the community, and to inquire about somewhere that might be available for rent. Unfortunately, nothing's available right now. There aren't any homes or apartments in town. So for the time being I'll be staying at the inn," Martha explained, not quite ready to bring up Mrs. Stavros's point that perhaps she'd be building a new home with Gray one day, if they did decide to marry.

Lucy look towards her husband, whose eyes twinkle with humor, seeming to already know where his wife was going with the conversation. She smiled at him, happy to see his approving look, before she turned back to her new business partner.

"With us going into business together, it's not sensible to have ya riding back and to town every day to conduct affairs. I think it would be best if ye stayed here with us till ya found yer own place. Then we could work together easier. Besides, I could use an extra hand around here, with me gettin' larger by the day," Lucy said, this time surprising Martha with an idea of her own. Martha was delighted by the offer, never having expected such kindness before.

"And you would have some of the same creature comforts as the hotel. We're the only other ones in the area to have indoor plumbing, and I even have an icebox. Keeps the groceries fresher longer," Sam said, seeming to boast, but Martha smiled nonetheless as Lucy giggled at him.

"Well, it sounds like I'd be quite foolish to refuse such an offer. I'd be happy to help you around the house, Lucy, and I'd be willing to pay expenses. I have a mare named Chestnut who I would be bringing with me, and I'm not going to be a freeloader, either," Martha said, a bit of sternness in her voice. She didn't want the Slaters to think that she'd ever abuse their hospitality.

"With ye starting the boutique for us, I'm sure we can work out some sort of agreement until ye find yer own living arrangements," Lucy said with a wink as she took another sip of her coffee.

Martha smiled, still having a hard time believing how fast her life was changing. And with that thought, the front door opened and in came the man she'd been hoping to see all day. Gray left his duster and hat at the door before he came into the dining room and took a seat next to Mary.

"Evening, ladies. Sam. How's the day been?" Gray asked, giving Martha a wink that brought a blush to her cheeks. She looked away from his warm eyes and focused on her coffee again.

"Spectacular!" Lucy said as she jumped right into everything she and Martha had been discussing. She was left quite winded by the time she'd finished, but she never stopped smiling excitedly the whole time she talked. Gray chuckled as he looked over at Mary, pleased to see how excited the two were, and to hear that Mary had found some sort of employment already, as long as the business was a success.

"And we've invited Mary to stay with us until she's settled elsewhere. I agree with Lucy that she could use an additional hand during the day, and the ladies will be able to conduct their business easier as well," Sam explained, giving Gray a pointed look. Gray smiled, but Sam could tell that he wasn't as thrilled about the idea as he'd though he would be.

"I'm sure you'll be more comfortable here with the Slaters than at the inn. And I know for a fact that Lucy will keep you busy," Gray said, turning his attention back to Mary.

She smiled up at him before saying, "I plan to come out tomorrow with Chestnut and my things. But would you mind giving me a ride back into town tonight?" Martha knew she could have asked Sam to hitch up the buggy and take her into town, but she was hoping to spend a little more time with Gray in private.

"I'd be happy to assist you back into town," Gray said, before turning to Sam. "Mind assisting me with hitching up the buggy, Sam?"

Sam was puzzled by the request, knowing that Gray was fully capable of doing it himself, but he appeased the man nonetheless. "Sure thing, Gray," he said as he rose and leaned over to give his wife a kiss on the check.

"I'll meet you out front when you're ready, Mary. Lucy, have a good evening," Gray said as he nodded to the ladies and left the ranch house with Sam in tow.

"Care to explain why a tough guy like you needs the help of a lowly doctor such as myself?" Sam asked as he followed Gray into the barn.

"Sam, what happens when Mary is living with you and the misses and things don't work out between her and me?" Gray said, spinning on his heel to look at Sam once they were alone in the barn.

Sam stopped and thought about it a moment, suddenly seeing Gray's perspective. "I honestly didn't think about that, Gray. She seems like such a sweet girl that I couldn't imagine you two not getting on together. She's full of energy, and she and Lucy really do have good plans for this boutique. She seems like a hard worker and seems very self-reliant. She told us about her leaving home and travelling all this way on her own," Sam said, hoping he hadn't offended his foreman and close friend.

"Sam, I have no doubt that she's all of those things and more. But I can tell that she's hiding something from her past, something that causes her to be hesitant any time we're about to have a moment. It's like she's scared to open up to me, and until she can be as open and honest as I've been with her, I can't guarantee that things are going to work out for me and her," Gray said with his hands on his hips, looking at the younger man.

Sam just nodded his head as he led a horse from its stall and towards the buggy. Gray didn't need the help, but he appreciated it at this moment. "I really do hope things work out between the two of you. I know it's a little early to tell, but you deserve to be happy, Gray, you really do," Sam said as he stood back to let Gray finish hitching up the buggy.

"I appreciate the words of support, Sam," Gray said as he finished up the work. Sam even held open the barn doors for him so he could drive the buggy up to the front porch where Mary was waiting for him. When Gray stopped in front of the ranch house, he hopped down and quickly moved to the other side of the buggy to help Mary into it.

"Thank you," Martha said as she got settled into the

buggy. She waved at Sam as Gray then drove the buggy away from the ranch. It was pretty dark out, but the light from the moon was enough to light the way. With the surrounding area being wide open, it was easy to get around at night as long as it wasn't too cloudy out.

"So, it seems like you've had a busy day," Gray commented, hoping to enjoy the ride into town with Mary.

"I feel like I've been living in a dream all day. I ran into Mrs. Stavros at the Eatery, and one thing led to another and she was taking us out here to the ranch to visit with Lucy. Then we talked business, Mrs. Stavros had to leave, and then we were getting dinner ready. It's like the day flew by, but so much happened at the same time that it's all rather hard to believe," Martha explained, still surprised by it all.

Gray chuckled as he looked down at the woman, her blue eyes seeming to shine even at night. He loved the way they sparkled in the sun, but at night they seemed absolutely dreamy. He thought about leaning down and kissing her, but wanted to wait until he could make sure she was ready for that sort of thing. "I'm sure glad to hear you've had a good day. I sure had fun ordering those Murtaugh boys all over the ranch. But I have to say, they're good workers even though they are absolutely green," Gray said with a shake of his head.

Martha laughed as she thought of how fast Eddie and Sawyer had moved to help Mrs. Stavros and herself down from the buggy the moment Gray had given the commend. "Well, I'm sure glad to hear they're not giving you any trouble and actually being of some use," Martha replied as she stared up at the sky, loving the view of all the stars. It was one of her favorite things to do at night because it made her feel like the sky was so large that anything was possible. Gray stole glances at her, thinking how beautiful she was and hoping that she was the one he'd been waiting for his whole life. But when he thought about her past, Gray knew that sooner or later they'd have to talk about it.

CHAPTER 14

*G*ray and Martha chatted idly, talking about Spruce Valley and all the people Martha had met that day. Gray joked about some of those people, and loved hearing the sound of her laugh, which seemed musical to him. When they came into town and headed towards the inn, he was enjoying himself so much that he didn't want the night to end. But he knew he needed to get back to the ranch and get some sleep, and more importantly find something to eat because he'd missed out on dinner. But when Gray noticed a small commotion outside the inn, he feared that his night wouldn't be over for some time.

"Oh, thank heavens, there you are, Miss Carver!" Bill Eckert exclaimed as Gray pulled the buggy up to the inn. Outside, Bill stood with Sheriff Ryder and Mrs. Royal, who looked quite pale and frightened.

"What's the matter?" Martha asked as Gray came around and helped her down from the buggy.

"I came to do my rounds in the rooms when I found your room door broken open and your things thrown around the room. I've feared the worst for you, Mary," Mrs. Royal explained, visibly shaken. Bill had an arm around the older woman, seeming to try to keep her calm.

"We were just giving a report to Sheriff Ryder before I sent Mrs. Royal home for the evening," Bill explained. "I was telling him how a young man came earlier this morning looking for a young lady matching your description, Miss Carver; but I didn't tell him anything, I swear. I don't know how he got past reception and into your room, if that is who done it."

Martha paled, fearing the worse. She swayed a little and Gray quickly steadied her, bracing her around the shoulders with his strong arms. Gray's warmth and grip around her brought some clarity to Martha's panicking mind. She didn't say anything, just stared ahead at Mrs. Royal, who seemed terrified.

The Sheriff finally spoke up. "Gray, why don't you take Greta home and I'll assist Mary with collecting her things."

Gray didn't want to leave Mary, but he knew that Josh probably wanted a minute alone with her to question her. He looked down at Mary and said, "You gather your things and I'll take you back out to the Slaters. Once we explain, they'll understand."

Martha just nodded her head, missing Gray's warmth as he stepped away from her and helped Greta up into the buggy. Then Martha went inside the inn with the Sheriff and Mr. Eckert.

"This way, Miss Carver," Mr. Eckert said, leading the trio

through the inn and upstairs to the rooms. As Martha took each step up, her heart beat faster and faster as she prepared herself for what she was going to find once she stepped into the room. As they neared the room, she could make out the mangled door that splintered into the bedroom. It appeared as though someone had rammed it.

Mr. Eckert stepped aside to allow Martha to enter first, and she placed her hand over her mouth once her eyes turned to the carnage in the room. Everything in the small room had been flipped over, torn apart, completely destroyed. As Martha stepped a few feet into the room, she surveyed the damage, thankful that she hadn't been present when the intruder came looking for her. Given the mayhem all around her, she was certain that, had she been in the room, she'd be dead by now.

"So, Bill, you said that no one noticed the break-in until Greta came upstairs to check on Miss Carver?" the Sheriff asked. Martha was making her way over broken furniture and torn bedding to reach the wardrobe, praying beyond hope that her one saddlebag still lay at the bottom. The doors of the wardrobe had been ripped off, as though the intruder had been in a rage, and nothing of hers now remained in it. Nothing but broken remnants.

"That's correct, Sheriff," she heard Mr. Eckert say as tears welled in her eyes. "I had Greta go check on Miss Carver this morning when the gentleman came asking about a young lady fitting Mary's description. When Greta said that Miss Carver was out for the day, I didn't think anything of it until this evening. Before Greta went home I had her check again, and that's when she saw what had happened. I can't believe it since I've been here all day, but with no other guests at the moment, I had no reason to go upstairs and check. I have no idea when this could have happened."

By now Martha was in shock and had started to tremble. Folding her arms around herself, she held onto herself as her eyes darted around the room. Not only were all her things either destroyed or missing, including the saddlebag with all the money in it, but she had a suspicion that she knew who had come looking for her.

Finding her voice, Martha asked, "What did this gentleman look like that came asking after me?" She turned her eyes towards the two men as they regarded her for a moment, clearly worried about her current state of mind.

"Well, he was taller than me, had very fair blond hair. He was wearing a western shirt and jeans, nothing fancy or out of the ordinary. He seemed friendly enough and didn't seem too upset when I lied to him about there not being a young lady here at the inn. I'm not sure how he found out," Mr. Eckert said as he started to ramble. The Sheriff was starting to worry about the fright everyone had had, but he also needed to do his job.

"Does that sound like anyone you know, Miss Carver?" Josh asked, observing Mary closely as she spoke.

Martha fixed her watery eyes on the Sheriff, doing her best not to cry or get overly emotional. After all, she'd been fearing this day ever since she ran away, and now that the day had come, she really shouldn't be surprised. She always knew in the back of her mind that her stealing that money would come back to haunt her, no matter how much good she tried to do with it.

"Yes, Sheriff, I do. His name is Jared Mathews. He's my

ex-fiancé," Martha explained. She knew the Sheriff would want more details, but she felt that could wait right now. After all, it was so late at night and she was suddenly feeling very exhausted.

"And do you believe that your ex-fiancé may want to cause you harm, Miss Carver?" the Sheriff asked, not liking the sound of where this burglary could be leading.

"Yes. I can think a few reasons why he'd want me dead," Martha said plainly, the tears finally spilling over onto her checks as the trembling increased.

All of a sudden, Gray was in the room, coming to her and wrapping his arms around her. Martha allowed the man to comfort her even though she felt she should have never come to Spruce Valley. How foolish she had been to think that she could ever settle down. The moment she found herself actually happy about the future was the moment her past came to haunt her.

"Shhh," Gray whispered into her hair as he held her tightly to his chest. "Everything is going to be okay. Let's get you back to the ranch and settled for the night."

Martha allowed Gray to lead her from the disaster of the room and back out into the chilly night air. She heard the Sheriff mention something about coming to speak with her tomorrow, but she didn't pay it any attention. She just wanted as far away from the inn as possible.

After helping her up into the buggy, Gray was quickly in the driver's seat, leading the horse out of town and down the main road towards the ranch. This time, they didn't say anything, although a million things ran through Martha's mind as she tried to reason what her next step was going to be.

Would Jared continue coming after her now that he'd gotten the money? Had Max sent him after her? Would she ever be able to escape them? When a fresh set of tears started to escape her eyes, Martha did her best to quiet her sobs the best she could.

Gray felt for the young lady, unable to imagine what it would feel like to have all your few possessions taken from you. He put an arm around Mary, pulling her close to him in hope of bringing her some sort of comfort. Gray felt a fury build up inside him towards the man that had caused Mary so much grief. It was becoming clearer to Gray what Mary may have been running from in the past, and he felt an undoubtable need to protect her.

As he led the buggy back to the ranch, he was starting to feel very determined about ensuring Mary's safety moving forward. Never had he felt this strongly about any woman before; though he'd spent very little time with Mary, he couldn't deny his feelings. One way or another he was going to make sure that he had Mary by his side for the rest of his life.

"Come now, Mary. We're almost home," Gray said softly, surprising them both as he used the term "home" instead of "the ranch". But he didn't regret saying it. Martha wrapped her arms around him, placing her head against his chest, allowing Gray to hold her close. "I'll not let any harm come to you, Mary. I promise you I'll always keep you safe."

Martha let the tears continue to fall, not because of the shock she'd experienced, but because of the relief that those words brought her. She was surprised when she felt the need to express her feelings for Gray. She had wanted to tell him "I love you", but quickly realized that it would be silly for her to say such a thing. Surely she couldn't be in love with this man already, even with his willingness to offer her protection? And though she had written to Gray with the intention of marrying him, she was still uncertain if she could ever love a man again. Martha was confused about the way she was feeling, but she knew one thing was for certain: she didn't want to let go of Gray.

When he stopped the buggy in front of the ranch house, Martha finally moved away from him. He was quick to come around and help her down, and with an arm around her shoulders he led her into the house.

"How did everything go this evening?" Sam called from the parlor, having stayed up to hear both Gray's evening report and any other interesting details of his and Mary's ride back into town. Honestly, he was dying to hear what Gray though of the young lady after getting to spend some genuine time alone with her. But as Gray came into the parlor leading Mary by the shoulders, Sam quickly stood, concerned to see Mary so upset.

"She was robbed, Sam," Gray said as he led Mary to his favorite chair by the fireplace and eased her down into the seat.

Martha didn't look up at Sam, feeling embarrassed about having to return sooner than expected, especially after how kind the Slaters had been to her. To bring this sort of trouble to Spruce Valley and to this ranch made her feel guilty. Jared could be very well watching her now and she felt the need to flee the house before anyone got hurt. For now, though, she needed to gather her wits about her.

"When we reached the inn, Josh was outside with Bill and

Greta. They explained that a man had come looking for Mary this morning, and later on her room was turned upside down. I don't think she was able to salvage anything," Gray explained, pulling a chair over to sit next to Mary, and slipping his hands into hers.

Sam couldn't deny the pleasure it brought him to see the way Gray was caring for Mary. The poor girl looked quite frightened, and he was glad that Gray had had the forethought to bring her back to the ranch. He just wished it was under different circumstances.

"I'm so sorry to hear this. Of course, Mary, you are welcome here. Lucy has already gone to bed, but I'm sure she'll be pleased to see you in the morning," Sam said kindly, taking a seat across from the couple. As he watched the two of them, both taking the time to look into each other's eyes, he was certain that they would indeed make a wonderful couple.

"Thank you, Sam. I'm indeed in your debt," Martha said softly, the trembling in her body seeming to return. She tried to hide it by letting go of Gray's hand and folding her own hands tightly together. But Sam noticed, his keen doctor's experience allowing him to see Mary more as a patient now than a house-guest.

"Gray, let's get Mary to the spare bedroom. I'm going to go prepare some laudanum to help her sleep tonight," Sam said, rising again and leading them to the spare bedroom once Gray had pulled Mary to her feet. He left them for a short while to prepare the tonic. Alone, Gray took a moment to turn down the comforter before leading Mary to the bed and easing her down upon it.

"I can manage, Gray. You don't need to fuss over me like a

child," Martha said in a shaky voice, trying to smile as she looked up at Gray, his onyx eyes seeming to shine in the dim light.

"I know I don't need to, Mary. But I want to," Gray said as he approached her, and, tilting her head towards his by lifting her chin, he placed his lips gently upon hers. Martha was shocked by the kiss, but she didn't move as she felt his warm lips on hers. It was soft and kind, neither needy nor demanding. It was so unlike anything she'd ever experienced before that all she did was focus on the feeling of how it made her feel and the warmth it seemed to fill her with. When Gray pulled away, it took Martha a second before she opened her eyes. She saw the way that Gray smiled kindly at her as he ran his fingers through her hair. He finally stepped away when they heard Sam coming back down the hallway to the room.

"Here you go, Mary. This will help you sleep," Sam said, noticing that her checks were now flushed. He had a suspicion that it had something to do with her and Gray being alone together for that moment; Gray's smile on his face was rather obvious, but the two made no mention of what had transpired between them as Mary took the medicine.

"Well then, I'll see you in the morning, then. Have a pleasant night, Mary. Gray, I would like a word within the parlor a moment," Sam said, nodding to Mary as he drew Gray from the room. Gray waved at Mary before closing the door behind him.

"Well, that sure was unexpected," Sam commented in a hushed tone once the two were in the parlor and away from the bedrooms. Gray plonked down in his chair and looked over at Sam, wishing he had his pipe on him. He ran his fingers through his hair, unable to get the thought of kissing Mary out of his mind.

"I knew she was running from something," Gray said as he finally took a deep breath and leaned back in the chair. "A young lady doesn't just up and leave because she's bored of where she lives and feels the itch to roam. A man – sure, I'd buy that story. But even with her father having passed on, surely she had no reason to leave everything she knew and was familiar with behind."

"And even with all of this happening, how does it make you feel about her?" Sam asked, unsure of how Gray was going to handle a young lady with such a mysterious past.

Gray looked up at Sam and a smile crossed his face. "I'll be honest, Sam, I kissed her in there. And it was unlike anything I've ever felt before. I've kissed my fair share of women, but nothing compared to that," Gray said, his smiling growing bigger as he admitted what he felt.

Sam couldn't help but smile and shake her head at Gray, not because he was surprised, but because he was relieved. It takes a certain type of man to take on a woman with a heavy past, and Gray proved that he could be a true gentleman even when he was also a hard-working ranch hand. Now they just had to discover what sort of past Mary was running from, and what they might be up against next.

"Why don't you go on and get some rest, Gray. Mary will be fine here and you can come check on her in the morning. I'm sure Josh will be out before too long, and I'm sure we'll have more answers as well," Sam said, knowing that it was getting rather late. He didn't want to be away from Lucy longer than he needed to; he felt his own need to put his arms around his wife and feel her close to him.

"You're right, Sam. Well, I'll see you in the morning, then," Gray agreed, standing and shaking hands with Sam before leaving out through the front door. Sam let out a long sigh as he blew out the lamps that were left on in the house when he'd waited up for Gray to return. He just wasn't expecting all of this to happen, and he sent up a silent prayer as he walked back to his and Lucy's bedroom, pleased to hear the house quiet once more.

CHAPTER 15

*W*hen Martha woke the next morning, her head was pounding, and as she opened her eyes it took her a moment to remember where she was. She lay still for several seconds, taking deep breaths and watching the sunlight dance around the room. It was a very stylish room, smartly designed, and the bed was rather comfortable, more so than the one at the inn had been. Memories of last night flooded her mind, and with it returned the fear that was sharp in her chest. The need to flee arose in her again and she worked very hard to tame those thoughts. After all, Chestnut was still at the livery stables back in town, and she now had no money to run with. No, Martha would have to face this day no matter what it would bring.

She sat up when she heard a knock on the door. Pulling the covers up over her chest since she only wore her chemise, she called for the person to come in. She was surprised when the door opened and Lucy popped her head in.

"Morning, Mary. I wanted to come in and check on ya," Lucy said, coming into the room and closing the door behind her. Then she crossed the floor and sat on the edge of the bed, taking Martha's hand in hers.

Martha tried to smile but failed, and focused instead on holding back her tears. "I just feel so embarrassed," she finally got out in a small voice. Saying how she felt out loud made it that much more difficult to hold back her tears. Lucy simply rubbed her hand, trying to comfort her new friend.

"Ye have nothing to feel embarrassed for, Mary. It's not like ya ask' that man to ransack yer room. And Sam and I already invited ye to come stay with us, so it's not like yer inconveniencing us or anything," Lucy said encouragingly. "And with me not fitting most of me gowns anymore, I'm sure we can find ya something lovely to wear today."

Martha couldn't help but smile as Lucy coaxed her from the bed and towards the wardrobe on the other side of the room. Opening the doors and drawers, Lucy picked out a lovely cream-colored day dress for Martha to wear, along with accompanying garments.

"You're too kind, Lucy," Martha said as she took the clothes and brought them over to the bed to lay them out.

"It's nothing at all, my dear," Lucy said with a wink. "Now, when yer ready, there's a certain man whose waiting for ya. But take yer time. The water closet is just across the hallway."

With that, Lucy left the room, giving Martha time to dress. Once she finished, she opened the door slowly, and seeing no one in the hallway, crossed to the water closet, taking her time to finish getting ready for the day. As she stood there pinning back her hair, not wanting to fuss to long with it, a feeling of sickness overtook her. Thankful to already be in the water closet, Martha vomited, sweat coating her forehead by the time it finally passed.

When the sickness left her and Martha washed her face, she took several deep breaths, trying to figure out why she'd been feeling so fatigued lately and been vomiting off and on. She wanted to speak to Sam about it right away – and then a thought sneaked its way into her mind. She did some quick thinking and adding up of recent weeks. Looking at herself in the small mirror in the water closet, her eyes grew big as she realized she hadn't had her monthly. Martha put her hand over her mouth as she fought the urge to cry as her worst fear came to mind. Surely it couldn't be true … could she be pregnant with Jared's child? After taking a deep breath, she opened the door and finally made her way to the main room.

Breakfast was well underway when she entered. Gray watched her as she came into the room, and moved down the bench to make room for her. She forced a smile at him as she took a seat and busied herself with fixing herself a plate. She wasn't hugely hungry but she knew that eating something would be important. She just wished she'd risen early enough to help Lucy with the meal; but she appeared well enough this morning, her laughter ringing through the air as they listened to Jensen tell a story about when he'd first learned to be a ranch hand.

"Sounds like Eddie and Sawyer." Gray spoke and then he took a long drink from his coffee. "Those two are so green that I'm surprised they made it through the day without spooking the cows or falling off their horses."

More laughter rang out, and for a moment Martha was able to forget all her worries. That was until Sam spoke up. "How'd you sleep last night, Mary? Any nightmares?"

Martha inwardly cringed as she tried to keep the smile on her face. "I slept fine, Sam, thank you. I appreciate the medicine." She felt like everyone was staring at her then, but Gray was quick to speak up.

"Time to move out, boys. I don't want to be sitting around when the Murtaugh boys show up. Jensen, I'm letting you take over things today. Surely there is no one better than you to show those two what to do," Gray said, standing from the table as he gathered his plate. Martha simply focused on her food, trying to eat something even though her stomach was in knots. She was pleasantly surprised when Gray stopped back at the table and placed a kiss on her cheek before continuing out the front door after the two other ranch hands. Martha's cheeks burned as she blushed, giving her face a fiery appearance, much like her hair.

"Well then, I'll leave you two ladies to it. I should be heading into town before my first patient of the day shows up," Sam said as he rose from the table.

"Sam," Martha called as she thought of something. "Could you bring Chestnut, my mare, back to the ranch with you this afternoon? I didn't have a chance to get her last night and I don't think I'll be going into town today."

"Certainly, Mary. I'd be happy to," Sam replied, bending over to give Lucy a kiss before he collected his doctor's bag and headed out of the house too.

"Well then, since we seem to have the house all to ourselves, why don't we make some oatmeal cookies," Lucy suggested happily. Martha chuckled as she set to work with the woman, busying themselves with chores and housework, chatting idly about the boutique and what they'd like to accomplish first. It was enough to keep Martha's mind off of worrying about possibly being pregnant.

~

GRAY HAD THOROUGHLY ENJOYED his morning watching Jensen bark orders at the Murtaugh Brothers while they were out in the field with the cattle. It seemed to breathe life into the old man to have something purposeful to do during the hectic calving season, and he was pleased to see the two young men following orders without issue.

When Gray noticed someone coming up the lane to the ranch house, he rode with haste to see who it was, intent on keeping his promise to Mary to always protect her. Though he'd had a good morning of working hard, his mind hadn't been very far from thinking about Mary and the kiss they'd shared the night before. As Gray got closer to the ranch house, he noticed that the rider was the Sheriff and figured he'd come by to ask Mary more questions about last night. Though Gray had his own questions, he was waiting for the best time to talk to Mary about them. But since Josh was here, he figured that now would be as good as any time with Jensen and Tom in the field with the two greenhorns.

"Afternoon, Sheriff," Gray called as he tied his horse's reins to the front porch post while the Sheriff rode over to him.

"Hello, Gray," Josh simply said as he dismounted. "I've come to ask Miss Carver some questions."

"I expected as much. I plan to join you," Gray explained as he led the man up the porch and into the house. They immediately smelled the aroma of baking and could only imagine that Lucy had made another batch of oatmeal cookies.

"Oh good. Now I won't have to eat them all meself," Lucy said as she came into the front room to see who'd come to visit. She'd gotten used to people coming and going in the ranch house, but she still never forgot the training Grant and Sam had given her when it came to using a gun. Granted, she didn't know how much help she'd be in her current state. "Mary and I made some cookies this morning and I've already had three!"

Gray chuckled, even more so when he saw the confused look on Josh's face. Gray led him to the parlor as Lucy disappeared and came back with Mary and a plate of cookies. Now understanding what Lucy was referring to, Josh took a cookie and thanked the ladies. He also watched Mary as she went and sat down next to Gray, who smiled at her.

"Good afternoon, Sheriff Ryder," Martha said, turning her focus back on him. Though she knew that the Sheriff had come to question her, it was also nice of Gray to take time out of his day to be with her too. Plus, it would make it easier to share her story with him, so that he would also come to understand her past as well.

"Afternoon, Mary. How are you doing today?" Josh asked, noticing how well she looked compared to last night.

"I'm fine, thank you," was all Martha said, waiting to take the Sheriff's lead.

"Well, I'm glad to see you are doing better. I'm sure last

night's events gave you quite a fright," Josh said, observing Mary closely.

"Indeed, Sheriff. I wasn't expecting anything like that to happen," Martha replied.

"Certainly. Now, Miss Carver, I have some interesting facts to share with you. Later last night, I was called down to Handy's – that's the local saloon in Spruce Valley. There had been some sort of ruckus there and a fight broke out over a card game. Unfortunately, a man was shot and killed. When I arrived to see what had happened, the man I found dead was a young man I'd never seen before, but he matches the description Bill gave of the man who'd come questioning about you," Josh explained, watching as Mary's eyes grew large with the news.

"Are you telling me Jared is dead, Sheriff?" Martha asked, her voice very soft. She didn't want to give up hope just in case the man he'd found dead wasn't Jared.

"If the details Bill gave me were correct – a tall man with blond hair, wearing a western shirt and jeans – then that would be the case. But unfortunately I'm going to need you to come to town and confirm the identity of the body," Josh said, hating to request such a thing from a young lady who was already shook up.

Martha took a deep breath as she nodded her head. "Absolutely, Sheriff. I'd need to know for myself anyways that it was him," she said, tears coming to her eyes. "I hate to say it, but it would surely bring me some peace to know that man was dead."

Lucy was surprised to hear her say this, wondering what she meant by those strong words. But it was Gray who spoke up next. "What did he do to you, Mary?" he asked softly, taking her hand in his. Martha didn't look at him, but enjoyed the feeling of his hand in hers. Since Jared was most likely dead, and the money now gone, Martha knew that she could leave out some details of her past and never have to speak or think about them again.

"I was a waitress at a restaurant in my hometown, so I met everyone that came in and out of our little area. A rodeo had come to town, and with it a bunch of different people. That is how I met Jared, one day at work when he came in for a meal right before the rodeo began. He was such a charmer, and his looks didn't hurt either. He was the first person I ever fell in love with, and after the rodeo ended he asked me to marry him," Martha began, still not meeting anyone's gaze as she talked. Instead she focused her eyes outside the window like she was watching her memories flash in front of her.

"I'd always wanted to leave that town behind, especially since my father had passed away and I didn't have any other family. I had a few friends, but there was no one I was willing to stay for. So I sold mostly everything I owned, including the ranch, and prepared to leave with Jared the next day. It was that night I found him in bed with another woman," Martha said, knowing she wanted to leave out the part where she was dumped in a hell-hole and sold as a slave. Her story didn't show Jared in any better light than what really happened, and by the time she realized that Gray was holding her hand tightly, she could only guess that her audience believed her.

"So I continued with my plan to go on this great big adventure that I'd had in mind when I agreed to leave with Jared; but after so many weeks I grew tired of it all. That's when I replied to Gray's ad in the paper and decided to make Spruce Valley my new home," Martha finished, hoping to be done talking about the whole situation. Surely with Jared dead, she no longer needed to worry about her past.

"I see, Miss Carver. Well, I certainly give you my sympathies concerning your plight. Mr. Mathews got what was coming to him when he chased you down and ransacked your room," Josh said, truly sorry for this young lady. But if Gray's actions had been any indication of his feelings, then Josh wasn't overly worried, feeling in his gut that Mary would be in good hands moving forward in her life.

"Thank you, Sheriff. I appreciate your kind words," Martha said. She let go of Gray's hand, then squared her shoulders. "I'd like to confirm the identity sooner than later. I want to get that part over with."

"Of course, Miss Carver. If you'd follow me back into town we can get this business over with," Josh said as he stood, placing his Stetson back on his head. Dealing with dead bodies was always the worst part of the job. But the sooner Miss Carver identified the corpse, the sooner everyone could move on.

"Would you like me to hitch up the buggy and take you into town?" Gray asked, wondering if she'd ever seen a dead body before. Then he chastised himself for such a foolish thought, knowing that both her parents had passed.

"I wouldn't want to inconvenience you, Gray. I know you must be getting back to your work and the other ranch hands," Martha reasoned, hating to take up any more of Gray's time. But he just smiled in return, a smile that seemed to melt the ice around her heart and make her head reason that perhaps she really could love again, especially now Jared was dead.

"I'll meet you out front, Mary," Gray said as he stood and followed the Sheriff out the front door.

"I'm so sorry for ya, Mary. I can't imagine what ye must be feelin' right now," Lucy said as she placed her hands on top of Martha's. She squeezed her friend's hand back and gave her a weak smile.

"To be honest, Lucy, it gives me much relief. I escaped his wrath and fate took care of the rest. I know it's not right to speak ill of the dead, but I'm glad that Jared Mathews is gone. He was a vile creature and I aim to make sure that the man that was shot is him," Martha said, with a stern edge to her voice.

"Well, yer a brave soul, Mary. Run along, then, and I'll see you after a bit," Lucy said, removing her hand and leading Martha out the front door. Lucy surprised her by embracing her, and when Martha looked into her eyes, she saw tears building. "Ah, don't mind me. I get a little emotional sometimes, that's all."

"I'll be back soon," Martha said with a smile as she descended the porch stairs and allowed Gray to help her back up into the buggy. She felt like she'd spent too much time riding around in the buggy with Gray, but she couldn't deny how happy she was to have him during this time in her life. Though it was rather strange to be riding into town to confirm the identity of her ex-fiancé with her prospective fiancé beside her; and while it also felt rather grim, Martha still couldn't suppress the small upwelling of happiness it brought her. Even with the chance that she was expecting.

CHAPTER 16

*A*fter taking care of things in town, with Martha confirming that the dead body was indeed Jared and adding to the Sheriff's report her statement of the events that transpired, she was looking forward to returning to the ranch with Gray. She had been so thankful to have him with her during the whole ordeal, and he'd been very patient with her when the sight of the body had brought her to tears. Now that they were heading out of town, Martha felt like she could breath again.

She was focusing now on what she planned to do for employment so she could replace the things that had been destroyed. She wouldn't be able to build a place of her own till she had saved quite a bit, and she didn't know how long the Slaters would allow her to stay with them. With a little one on the way, she didn't imagine it could be very long. Martha sighed deeply as she tried to figure out what she was going to do. If she was expecting a little one in a few short months, she would have to secure her future and that of her child.

"A penny for your thoughts?" Gray spoke up, noticing the way Martha looked anxious and confused. But that all seemed to go away as she looked up at him and smiled. That sight alone made him want to lean over and kiss her silly. But he refrained, genuinely curious as to what she was thinking about.

"Well, in the end, Jared really did take everything from me, and I don't think I'll be getting any of it back. I know I need employment, and I don't know how long the Slaters will allow me to stay with them. Getting the boutique open and running it with Lucy will take time since she's expecting ... and now that I'm penniless I may need to start looking for other work," Martha explained, knowing that her situation didn't really paint her in a good light for Gray. She wondered what he thought of her now that all of this had happened. The thought caused her to look away from him: she had starting to feel ashamed all over again.

"Don't," Gray said, putting the reins in one hand so he could use the other to pull her chin up to him, forcing her to look at him. "I can see the anxiety in your eyes, Mary. But I'm telling you that you don't have to worry. Now, all your problems can't be solved today, but rest assured I won't let anything happen to you. We can do this together."

"Together?" Martha said softly, her eyes growing wide at the thought. Could Gray really still care for her after learning so much about her past? But the guilt overthrew any joy she could feel, knowing that there was still plenty she could tell Gray about herself – including her real name. Her face softened as she looked into his onyx eyes, wishing she could simply believe in his words and not feel so much turmoil inside of her.

"I know we haven't known each other that long, Mary, but I can't deny these strong feelings I have about you. You're beautiful, brave, funny, and, most importantly, open-hearted. If you can accept a man like me, someone whose always been considered the bad boy in town, then there is no reason why I wouldn't accept you for who you are," Gray said, a moment before he lowered his lips to hers, claiming her mouth in a hungry kiss that was full of passion and wanting. Martha wrapped her arm around his torso, pulling herself closer to him to deepen the kiss. She'd never wanted anything more than to forget the guilt and just feel the love for this man that was waiting to take hold of her. She wanted to create a new life with Gray, one not full of fear of the past, and she was practically desperate to make that happen.

They quickly parted when they felt the buggy wheel roll off the edge of the road, causing Gray to jerk and lead the horse back into the middle. Martha couldn't help but laugh as she stayed close to Gray, her arm still wrapped around him. Soon they were laughing together, both surprised at how their emotions had gotten the best of them.

"For now, Mary, we just take it one day at a time," he said, leaning his head against hers.

"Alright, Gray. I can do that," Martha replied, for now just enjoying the feeling of him close to her, allowing her, in this moment, to forget about the past or the future.

When they got back to the ranch, Martha headed into the house while Gray took the buggy to the barn to unhitch the horse and get back out to the pasture to help wrap up the tasks for the day. He missed being around his woman, but knew he'd already spent too much time away from his work to justify staying close to her the rest of the day. Gray enjoyed that thought – *his* woman – as he went about his work.

Martha, on the other hand, was all over with her emotions. She couldn't deny any longer that she had strong feelings for Gray – but how was he going to react when she told him her real name and why she'd lied to everyone? She knew that she couldn't really move forward until she completely confessed her past. And what would Gray say when she told him her fear that she was pregnant. As she thought about the passionate kiss she'd shared with him earlier, she knew that she couldn't wait much longer to tell him the truth before they became any more serious in their relationship. There were so many promises in Gray's words that she felt she had to do right by him, no matter what.

Martha was busy helping Lucy tidy up the house and prepare dinner when she noticed a few figures out of the corner of her eye. Thinking they must be the ranch hands, Martha moved over to the window and gasped when she saw instead three Indians nearing the ranch house.

"Lucy!" Martha called as she ran to the kitchen. "Tell me you have a gun in this house. There's three Indians coming up to the house."

"Oh Mary, I'm so sorry, me dear. Ye must not be used to Indians and I didn't tell you about the local tribe here that Sam is friendly with. I'm sure they're just Red Dog's friends,"

Lucy said, trying to be reassuring. "They can be quite a fright when yer not used to seeing them." She patted Martha on the shoulder, who was still somewhat stunned but had the nerve to follow Lucy to the front door as a knock came upon it.

When Lucy opened the door, three tall Indian men stood on the other side. And as Martha watched Lucy smile at them, she tried to not look as frightened as she felt. Not only were they tall, intimidating, with long, flowing black hair and dark eyes, but they also wore nothing more than breechcloths, although one had on a few necklaces that seemed to be made out of horsehair and small bones.

"Hau, Lucy Slater. I've come with my sons to bring you payment for the sheep," the man in the middle said, his eyes shifting between Lucy and Martha. "I hope we are not interrupting."

"No, Bright Star, yer always welcomed. I'm glad to hear that Drake and Robert Red Dog delivered the sheep to ye," Lucy said, stepping back and allowing the men to enter the house, something that caused Martha to tense. She had no idea that the Slaters did business with Indians, and she'd never met one before. "May I introduce ye to Miss Mary Carver."

When Lucy said her false name, Martha shifted her eyes to the ground as she nodded her head. She didn't want their eyes on them. But when the older man spoke again, the one that Lucy had called Bright Star, she couldn't help looking up at him as he said her name. "Miss Mary Carver, I am pleased to meet you. May you know my sons, Running Bear and Sky Bird."

Martha looked over at the two Bright Star had introduced, and nodded her head towards them, watching as the two younger men regarded her. It made her feel uneasy, the way they watched her, and she was even more surprised when Bright Star began to laugh.

"Forgive me, Miss Mary Carver, and my sons. We have never seen anyone with such beautiful red hair before," Bright Star explained, making his sons look away from Martha and instead begin to look at their own feet. Martha then understood that their father had embarrassed them. "Your husband will surely be a lucky man."

This made Martha blush, as she realized that Bright Star was flirting with her, which then caused Lucy to laugh. "You'll be pleased to hear that she is being courted by Gray Jenkins," Lucy said, humor in her eyes.

Bright Star raised his eyebrows as he regarded Martha again. "But Miss Mary Carver, Gray Jenkins has seen many seasons. Surely my young sons would be of more interest to a beautiful young girl such as yourself," he said, a smile on his lips. Martha couldn't help but laugh then, especially when one of the sons grunted in response to what his father had said.

"As kind an offer as that is, Bright Star, and though I mean your sons no dishonor, I do quite enjoy Gray's company," Martha said in Gray's defense. She was at least more at ease now that she'd seen how well Bright Star spoke English and his quick humor.

"Well then, on to other matters. Lucy Slater, we bring you moccasins that my younger sister made, in hopes of bring your relief during your pregnancy," Bright Star said, motioning to one of his sons, who pulled out a pair of moccasins from the small satchel he carried and handed them over to Lucy.

"These are very beautiful, Bright Star. Please tell Red

Feather I said thank you," Lucy said as she felt the fur inside the moccasins, and then handed them to Martha to feel. She was surprised by how soft they were, and thought they'd feel lovely on the feet.

"I also bring this knife that I made myself this past winter when the nights were long and cold," Bright Star said, unsheathing a knife from his side and handing it carefully to Lucy, the hilt being made out of what looked like bone. "The handle is made from buffalo bone, and the knife from iron ore that I had treaded the summer before. It's good for cutting and slicing many things."

"Yer very talented, Bright Star. I will show Sam when he gets home later today, but I don't know if I'll let him have it," Lucy said, causing them all to chuckle as she laid it carefully on the dining table. "Can I offer ye any tea?"

"No, Lucy Slater. We must be returning to our camp. I want you and Sam Slater to know how grateful we are to have the extra meat till we can go buffalo hunting," Bright Star said as he motioned to his sons, who made their way to the front of the house once again.

"Of course, Bright Star. We are happy to do business with the Crow Tribe. If I wasn't expecting, I'd come visit the next time Sam pays ye a visit," Lucy said as they all stepped out onto the front porch.

"When your little one comes along, please bring it to the camp. I'll do a special blessing for your child, Lucy Slater," Bright Star said before turning to Martha. "It was nice to meet you, Miss Mary Carver. Gray Jenkins is a lucky man." He winked at her then, making Martha blush as the Indians stepped off the porch and made their way down the lane, Lucy standing and waving at them as they left.

"Well, that was rather unexpected," Martha commented as the two went back inside the house. She let out a heavy sigh as she began to chuckle. "I never expected to ever be flattered by an Indian." She and Lucy laughed together as they began preparing for dinner.

CHAPTER 17

artha had gone out to the pasture to watch the cattle roam as the sun was setting. She'd enjoyed helping Lucy with dinner and was so pleased when Sam had returned to the ranch with Chestnut in tow. She was undoubtedly grateful for everything the Slaters had done for her. She enjoyed laughing over dinner as Lucy told the story of the Indians coming to visit and how terrified Martha had been. She'd even enjoy teasing Gray when she told him about Bright Star offering his sons as a possible husband. They all enjoyed the banter that passed back and forth between everyone, making Martha feel like she was a part of a family again.

She'd never had a large family, but she missed the way she'd laugh with people she cared about. Her mother had passed away when she was little, but her father always made her feel a part of a family, making her laugh and feel loved. She was glad to be a part of something like that again. But deep down inside, she knew that if it was going to last, she'd have to come clean with all of them.

Martha turned when she heard footfall behind her. She smiled as she looked up at Gray coming towards her, the setting sun shining off his hair, making him appear to have a halo. He looked angelic in that moment, despite his womanizing ways in the past. There was nothing Gray had shown her thus far that convinced her otherwise.

"I wondered where you'd run off to," Gray said as he joined her, leaning against the fence as he cast his gaze over the pasture. He spotted several newborn calves, and felt a sense of pride in knowing he helped those little animals come into this life.

"I just needed a bit of fresh air. I sort of needed to catch my breath after all that laughing I did," Martha explained as she followed his gaze, smiling as she watched the mama cows fuss over their newborns.

Gray chuckled as he thought of the jokes that had been told. "Yeah, it's not normally that rowdy. But you seem to bring the best out in us," he said as he looked down at Mary, his heart filling with pride for her as well. He was truly proud to think of her as his woman, and in turn he began to think about how much longer he'd wait before he proposed. It was obvious to him that they had great chemistry, and he loved everything he'd learned about Mary, even though she'd had some hard patches in her life when it came to love. And despite all that, she'd seem to be opening up to him and try for love again.

"You're too kind, Gray," Martha said, her smile slipping away as she turned back towards the pasture and leaned up against the fence. She sighed, knowing that now would be as good a time as any to talk to Gray about the truth.

"I've seen that look before, Mary. I have a feeling you're about to tell me something that's been heavy on your shoulders. Let me just say now that there isn't nothing in your past that would make me stop feeling the way I feel about you, even if you tell me you're not a virgin," Gray said, trying to ease whatever was bothering her.

Martha smiled for a moment before saying, "What? Are you telling me that you are?"

They both laughed at that, but Martha's smile soon slipped away again. "Just tell me, Mary," Gray urged, coming close to her then.

"Gray, my name's not Mary," Martha started with, figuring that was one of the biggest lies she'd told yet. Gray's eyes narrowed at her and he stilled, running what she'd said through his mind once more. "My name is Martha Walters. Ever since I ran away, I've been telling people my name is Mary Carver so that I wouldn't be found. But I guess that didn't quite work out."

Gray didn't say anything as she talked. He was stunned by this news even though he understood why she'd lied. She had been trying to hide from her ex, and a new name would help. "But why didn't you at least tell me the truth … Martha?" Gray asked, her real name unfamiliar on his tongue.

"Needless to say, I have a hard time trusting anyone, after what I went through," Martha continued. "And it's a lot more than what I told Sheriff Ryder this morning." She went on to tell him everything. How not only had she'd fallen in love with Jared, sold everything, and left with him, but how she'd been sold by Jared to a heinous man named Max and been expected to serve him and the patrons of his saloon. Her voice became strained as she told Gray how she'd escaped, and the money she'd stolen to pay her way these last four weeks.

The whole time she spoke, Gray didn't say a word. He simply watched her as she told him everything, a new person seeming to appear right before him. Martha wasn't just brave – she had risked her life to be where she was today. But the more she talked, the more he began to fear. First, if Jared was able to finder her, who was to say that this Max guy mightn't, too? And second, if she could lie this much to him and others, did that mean she would lie to him in the future to try to cover up other things she'd do?

Gray's demeanor darkened right before her eyes. She could tell that what she'd just told him wasn't settling all that well. Martha didn't blame him, because she knew it was a lot to take in. She knew the risk of telling him would possibly undo everything he felt for her. And by the almost angry look he gave her, she was certain that any future they might have had was now over with.

"Why did you tell me all of this now?" Gray asked, his voice shaking with all the emotion he was feeling. Half of him wanted to pull her into his arms, and the other wanted to tell her to never talk to him again.

"Because you deserve to know everything there is about me, Gray. I have strong feelings for you and wanted you to know all this before things become official between us. In your letter you stated how you wanted complete honesty, and you'd been so honest with me that I felt so guilty keeping any of this from you. And to make matters all the worse, since this morning I've feared that I might be pregnant. I've been feeling awful in the mornings and I haven't had my monthly," Martha explained, looking down at her feet.

Gray considered her words as the shock of it all rolled over him, looking off in the distance before focusing back on her again. "So you were intimate with Jared, then?" Gray asked softly, seeing the way she trembled before him. He wanted to wrap his arms around her but didn't know if that would be the right thing to do. It was one thing to want a wife. It was another to want to become a father so soon after marriage.

Martha just nodded her head, unable to look up at Gray as she confirmed one of the most horrible aspects of her past: the fact that she hadn't waited till she was married to give that special part of herself to someone else.

"I need some time to think about all of this, Martha. It even feels strange saying your real name. And the Slaters are going to need to know as well, especially if this Max comes looking for you, and his money," Gray said in an even tone, trying to keep his composure. Speaking those words made him think of something else Martha hadn't explained yet. "And how much money are we talking about anyways?"

Martha swallowed hard as she looked away, unable to meet Gray's eyes. "About fifty thousand dollars in large bills," she said softly.

Gray felt like the wind had been knocked out of him. He was surprised that Martha was still alive given the sheer amount she'd been carrying. If Max hadn't tracked her down yet, he was going to do everything in his power to get that kind of money back. And if Jared had already found her, Gray was quite certain Max would, too, if he hadn't already.

"And you don't have it anymore, correct?" Gray asked, hating to see Martha this upset again. But he couldn't let his feelings dictate his actions right now. No, right now he needed to keep a level head about him.

"No. Jared took it when he raided my room and destroyed my things," Martha confirmed, still not looking back into Gray's eyes.

"Well then, we better go tell the Slaters together," Gray said, knowing that his employers would need to know the type of threat they could be under with Martha being such a large target for what she'd done. However, he still wasn't going to allow any harm to come to her. He held out his hand towards her, but she didn't take it.

"I just need another few moments, Gray," Martha said, folding her arms around her.

"Sure, I understand," he said, stepping back from her before turning and heading back towards the ranch house.

Martha watched him walk across the lawn and go back into the house. She feared having the conversation with the Slaters and wondered if they'd kick her out, knowing that she could be putting them all in potential danger. Surely Sam wouldn't allow such a thing to happen to his expecting wife.

Wanting to seek comfort and strength before she went into the ranch house, Martha headed towards the horse barn, ducking inside the door and seeking out her mare in the dim light of the setting sun. The light was so poor that even though she found Chestnut easy enough, she didn't hear or see the person who snuck up behind her and struck her on the back of the head until she was unconscious.

CHAPTER 18

*G*ray paced the parlor waiting for Martha to arrive to talk to the Slaters with him. He wasn't about to tell her story for her, but he had let Sam and Lucy know that they needed to talk to them. At first Sam was excited at the prospect of Gray sharing the news that he'd proposed, even though it seemed a little soon; but by the grave way that Gray looked, Sam knew it wasn't good news. Lucy had put on a kettle of tea, and when it began to whistle she went to get it from the stove.

"I'll go see if she's okay," Gray said. He looked over at Sam before quickly leaving the ranch house once again. He went back to the spot he'd last seen her, the night having set in and the dark making it hard to see clearly. When he didn't find her near the pasture, he went to the barn and lit a lamp. Holding it above his head, he looked around and found her mare still in her stall, so he knew that Martha hadn't left. But when he looked down at the floor, he gasped to see blood near the mare's stall.

Moving quickly, Gray ran back to the ranch house, cursing himself for ever leaving Martha alone, especially after everything she'd told him about this Max fellow. Bounding up the steps, he barged in through the front door and went straight to the parlor, telling Sam and Lucy in a hurry everything Martha had told him, plus the fact that he now suspected that she'd been kidnapped.

"I'll ride to town and warn Josh. Gray, ride to the Indian camp and tell Bright Star. He's the best tracker I know and will surely help us," Sam said as he rose. He then turned to Lucy and kissed her softly. "Go get Tom and Jensen to come stay up at the house while we're away. Sleep with the shotgun tonight and make sure to give Tom and Jensen a pistol from the safe."

"Don't ye worry about me. Just go out there and bring that girl home," Lucy said with tears in her eyes at the thought of someone harming Mary … Or rather Martha, she corrected herself.

"I will, my dear, don't you worry about that," Sam said as he followed Gray out the front door, both men ready to take action.

As Martha came to, she felt sore all over. The back of her headed pounded and her arms and legs felt stiff. When she tried to open her eyes, she was blinded by the light around her. Blinking back tears, she was able to discover that the light was only from a single candle, yet it hurt her eyes immensely. She didn't try moving but simply looked around her, realizing she'd been taking from the barn and tied to a chair in a small cabin she didn't recognize. She tried to keep her breathing steady, but she was truly scared.

"Looks like my little darling is awake," came a chilling voice from across the room. Martha hadn't seen him in the shadows, but as Max leaned forward in his chair, she could see the candlelight highlighting his face. Just like the first time Martha had met the man, when she had at first thought Jared had just taken her to a random saloon for a drink and dancing, Martha thought Max looked quite handsome, with his black hair parted to the side and his moustache grown long enough that he could twist the ends. But it didn't take Martha long to realize that Max was really the devil disguised as a gentleman. One moment she'd been having the time of her life, and the next she been abandoned and sold by her lover. Looking into his eyes now, Martha feared for her life.

"Now that you're awake and we have no one to bother us, let's get down to business," Max said as he stood up and crossed the little room, standing above her so that Martha had to look up at him, the action causing her head to swim with pain. "Where is my money, you piece of filth?" He spat on her, making Martha recoil. She felt disgusting just being in his presence.

"Jared took it when he tore apart the room I had been renting at the inn in town. It was gone when I returned, so I figured he had it," Martha explained. She wasn't expecting him to lash out and strike her, so when he did, she cried out in shock and pain.

"You can scream all you like, Martha dear, because no one is around for miles to hear you. And unless you want me to hit you again and give you a real reason to scream, I suggest you tell me the truth," Max said as he knelt down in front of her. "Jared didn't have the money on him when I shot him dead. After my men searched him, his horse, and the filthy room he'd been sharing with a whore, they found nothing. So, unless he buried it somewhere, you must still have it."

The room swirled as Martha tried to look into Max's eyes, but she was having a hard time staying conscious after that last hit. She wanted to vomit and pass out at the same time and wasn't sure she had the strength to do either. "I don't know where the money is, Max, I swear. I promise I'll pay you back, just let me go," Martha said softly, wishing there was some way she could escape this hell all over again. She tried to focus on Gray's face to give her comfort, but it only brought tears to her eyes as she thought about the fact that she'd probably never see him again.

"It would take years for you to pay back what you stole from me, you wench. So, you can either tell me where the money is or I'm going to end you right here," Max said, his voice rising until he was practically yelling at Martha. He slapped her again, this time sending backwards the chair in which she was tied, and as her head collided with the floor she thankfully slipped into unconsciousness again.

CHAPTER 19

"Are you sure this is the place?" Gray whispered to Bright Star. The Indian nodded his head as they all fixed their eyes on the structure in front of them, a dim light glowing from within. They were crouched down together in the tall grass surrounding the abandoned cabin Bright Star had led them to. Behind them were Sheriff Ryder and Sam, both intent on helping them out on this mission. When Gray had reached Bright Star at the Crow Indian Camp, Bright Star had listened intently to Gray's plight and had agreed to aid the man. And since Bright Star was known as the best tracker in camp, he'd left with Gray as soon as the rancher had finished explaining what had happened.

They'd started their search at the barn, and with his years of experience tracking wounded animals, Bright Star had been able to lead the small search party to an abandoned cabin in the woods – or at least believed it was abandoned. Josh was already making mental plans to have the cabin dismantled once they'd successfully rescued Martha. Having been filled in on Martha's full history, he was as intent as Gray on rescuing the young woman. He couldn't imagine being betrayed like Martha had by the one she thought she'd loved.

"Looks like there's only one way in," Josh said softly, only seeing a front door and a single window. He didn't know who owned the property, but he assumed the cabin had been created for hunting in the winter: just enough shelter to provide a man the bare minimum while away from home.

"I agree," Sam joined in, his pistol in one hand and his medical bag in the other. He didn't know what condition they were going to find Martha in, but he was intent on keeping the promise to his wife to bring the woman home.

"Josh and I will go in the front. Sam and Bright Star, hang here in case we need back-up," Gray said, his eyes searching the only window for signs of Martha, silently praying she was still alive. He didn't want to think about what might have happened to her since he'd last seen her by the pasture. It felt like an eternity ago.

"When you're ready, Gray," Josh said, moving up close to Gray as everyone took their positions. Gray wasn't a gunfighter, but he was ready to do everything that was possible to rescue the woman he'd fallen in love with. That thought alone fuelled his determination to see Martha well again, and, more importantly, in his arms where she belonged.

Gray and Josh moved slowly up to the front door, listening for any sounds around them. They didn't know how many men were in the cabin or if anyone was patrolling the grounds round about. They stood still by the door for a moment, trying to hear anything that would give them an advantage, but when the night's silence was pierced by Martha's screams, Gray lost all patience and kicked in the door, firing a warning shot at the ceiling as he barged into the small room, Josh right behind him.

Upon hearing the gun firing, Max darted behind Martha and crouched there as though she was his shield. He held a knife up to her neck as his eyes darted back and forth between the two men who'd ruined his torture session, something he quite enjoyed doing in his spare time.

"Drop the knife or you're dead," Gray shouted, trying to aim his gun at the man who held his precious Martha at knife-point. He didn't want to accidently shoot Martha, but the man wasn't giving him an easy opening.

"Back off or the girl dies," Max replied with a sneer, his cold voice sending chills down the spines of the other men. They both understood that this evil man wasn't lying when he made that threat.

Martha's vision swam as she tried to focus on Gray's face. She'd lost all hope of being rescued when Max had woken her once again, the pounding in her head growing more severe with every passing second. Martha felt the cold steel across her neck and did her best to keep her head up, even though it felt like it weighed a hundred pounds. She struggled between staying conscious and not slicing her own neck on the blade. Either way, she prayed that it would all be over soon.

"Just give up now, you vile scum. The cabin's surrounded and you're not getting away with kidnap and attempted murder," Josh shouted, growing anxious with every passing second. They were at a standoff, with Martha's life hanging in the balance.

Suddenly, gunfire rang out from the distance, a bullet piercing the only window, making Max shift his position, his line of thinking being that the attack was now coming from outside. But the moment the man moved, Josh and Gray took their shots, too, moving forward as Max hit the floor hard. Josh was on him within a second, sending another shot into the man's right arm to prevent him from firing back at them. When Max tried to stab Josh in the ankle with the knife boot he'd unsheathed, Josh jumped out of the way and sent another bullet into the man, finally ending all movement.

Gray ignored the kidnapper and turned his attention to Martha. Tears streamed down her face as he whispered comforting words to her, despite the two further gunshots that rang out beside them. Sam and Bright Star had come in now, and Sam was quick to help Gray get Martha untied. Collecting Martha in his arms, Gray walked her out of the cabin, Sam close behind him as he started to examine her.

"Let's get her to the clinic in town. It's closer," Sam said, unable to see Martha's wounds clearly in the dark. "You get her into the buggy and I'll drive."

Gray didn't reply but did as he was told. His biggest concern now was to get Martha to safety and allow Sam to make sure she'd live through this ordeal. If Martha died on him now, Gray was certain he'd live the rest of his life a vary sad and angry old man.

THE FIRST THING Martha realized as her mind came out of the darkness of her subconscious was that she was warm. She took a deep breath; the smell of wildflowers was close by. It reminded her of spring, which helped her remember that it was March and that there shouldn't be wildflowers in bloom right now, and then that triggered her last memories of Max torturing her to death.

Her eyes shot open and she tried to sit up from where she was lying, but the pain in the back of her head made it hard for her to focus her eyes or gain balance. She felt a pair of hands on her, urging her to lie back down. She fought against the hands until she heard her name from a familiar, comforting voice.

"Martha, you need to lay down. You must get some rest," Gray said, his touch warm on her skin where he pressed his hands into her shoulders, forcing her to lie back down and relax.

"Where am I?" she asked, the words hard to say because her mouth was so dry, as though she'd swallowed a spoonful of dirt before falling asleep.

"You're safe, Martha. After we rescued you, Sam and I took you back to Sam's clinic. You're there now, resting after sustaining several head injuries," Gray explained, speaking slowly and softly, his words causing fear to run through her again as she remembered the way Max had hit her over and over again.

Martha felt Gray's hand on her head then, gently tipping her head up as he placed a cup to her lips, allowing her to drink deeply of the water. When she'd finished, he laid her down again gentle as a feather. Martha swallowed several times and then took a deep breath as she struggled not to cry or get upset. Her head already hurt as it was, and she was still trying hard to focus on Gray. She looked towards him but only saw the blur of a figure.

"What happened to Max?" she asked, not remembering much after Gray and Josh had stormed the cabin. She didn't want to think about the vile man ever again, but the fear wouldn't allow her to be free yet.

"He's dead, Martha. Josh killed him after Max tried to stab him. You won't ever have to worry about him again," Gray said, taking her hand as the tears finally came down her checks. She felt relieved to know that Max was dead and wouldn't be able to hurt her again. "Shhh, my love. You don't have to worry about him now."

Through Martha's tears, she was still able to hear Gray clearly. "You love me?" Martha asked between sobs, having a hard time believing anyone would love her after everything she'd been through.

"Yes, Martha," he said, coming closer to her. "I love you, and I'm never letting you out of my sight again."

Before Martha could say anything in returning or declare her own deep feelings for the man who'd captured her heart, she felt Gray descend upon her, his lips capturing her as his free hand wiped away her tears. He was gentle and Martha was hungry for more, but the pounding in her head wouldn't allow her to lift her head and press harder against Gray. Sensing her discomfort, Gray pulled away.

"I love you, too, Gray. I never thought I could ever love a man again after the betrayal I experienced, but I know that what I feel for you is like nothing I've ever felt before. I feel safe with you, Gray, and I want to spend the rest of our lives together," Martha said slowly, wishing she could see more clearly. "But what if I'm pregnant, Gray? Surely you wouldn't want to take on a child that isn't yours?"

Gray took a deep breath as he squeezed Martha's hand again. "I'm so glad to hear you return my feelings, Martha. And yes, I love you even if you are pregnant. I want to have children with you Martha, and I think the sooner the better," he said, the smile apparent in his voice.

Martha cried happy tears as she clung to Gray, feeling happier than she had in years. But then she frowned, becoming frustrated with her lack of sight. "Gray, is Dr. Slater nearby? I'm having trouble seeing and I don't understand why," she said, reaching out towards Gray till she could at least touch his face.

"Of course, Martha. You just rest here. I'll go get Sam," Gray said, placing a light kiss on her forehead as he let go of her hand and left her side. Martha took several deep breaths as she closed her eyes and opened them again, hoping that her vision would clear and she'd be able to see Gray's face again.

After a while, she heard footsteps near the small bed. She tried to look over at who was approaching her but still failed to see clearly. It was a little disturbing, but she relaxed once she heard Sam's voice.

"Good morning, Miss Walters," Sam said, the humor apparent in his voice.

"Hello, Sam," Martha replied as she felt Sam approach her, his hand gentle on her shoulder as he moved her hair this way and that, as though inspecting her head.

"You've taken a nasty beating, Martha," Sam said, analyzing the bruising that had formed across her scalp, the sides of her face, and the swelling on the back of her head where she sustained multiple blows to the head. "Do you feel any pain?"

"Yes, Sam. My head feels like it's pounding," Martha admitted.

"I'm going to prepare some laudanum to help ease the pain, but only a little bit since we're all pretty sure your pregnant," Sam explained, and Martha soon heard the opening of a bottle and the clanking of a metal spoon against the glass. When she felt it pressed against her lips, she parted them and drank the bitter medicine quickly, praying it would work fast. "It's going to make you sleepy and you'll probably fall asleep soon, but that's okay because you need your rest. We won't know if there is any permanent damage to your eyes until you've rested for a few days. For now, try to rest and not worry about anything. You have a guardian angel beside you who's informed me that he's not leaving your side till you're full recovered."

They chuckled as Martha felt the effects of the laudanum kick in. She felt it easier to laugh now, even though the effort caused her head to swim. Her vision continued to blur until her eyes were closing, and as her breathing became steady, she felt someone take her hand. She focused on the texture of the calluses of the man's strong hands as she fell back to sleep.

CHAPTER 20

*I*t had taken Martha a week in the clinic until she was fully recovered from the beating she'd endured. Sam once told her that it was a miracle that she'd not only lived but had very few injuries besides severe bruising. With time, her vision had cleared and she could see properly again. She had spent her time praying words of thanks and thinking about how she'd live each day to the fullest, never taking a moment for granted.

Now back at the ranch house with the Slaters, Martha was almost feeling her old self, despite the morning sickness. She enjoyed working with Lucy every day, whether it was house-work, ironing out the details of the boutique, or talking about their pregnancies. Already Lucy had written her family contacts back in Buffalo, New York for advice on the latest fashions and fabrics that would be suitable for pioneer women. It wouldn't be long before Lucy had everything she needed to start filling her boutique with the things the women of Spruce

Valley desired. It was up to Martha then to find the perfect store front and start getting it ready.

Though Martha no longer had a cent to her name, she was happy to work with the Slaters in return for the things she needed. And one of the biggest perks of going into business with Lucy and staying with the Slaters was that she got to see Gray on a daily basis. Even though they'd confessed their love for each other, they were taking things slow so they could enjoy this newfound feeling for each other. Gray reasoned that he wanted to court Martha properly with no fear or lies to get in the way of what they wanted to build together. And every day that Martha got to spend some time with Gray was what she considered Heaven must be like.

She was doing the lunch dishes while Lucy was lying down for a nap, fatigue seeming to get the best of her during this last portion of her pregnancy, when Martha heard a knock on the front door. Drying her hands on her apron, she left the dishes and went to the door, and was pleasantly surprised to see Greta on the step. But as Martha looked the widow over, her eyes grew wide as she realized what Greta had slung over her shoulder.

Martha quickly pulled Greta inside, fear clenching her chest as she looked at the woman with confusion written across her face. "Mrs. Royal, where on earth did you find that saddlebag?" Martha demanded as she led Greta into the parlor and sat her down in a chair, Martha's chest rising and falling as she tried to control her breathing.

"Please don't be displeased with me, Miss Walters, but you have to understand that I didn't steal it. After that man came asking for you, I knew that I needed to get it to a safe place. I'm sorry I wasn't able to rescue all your things, but I knew that this would be important to you. And with you ending up bedridden for so long, I knew that wasn't the best time to tell you. But now that you're settled and well, I thought you'd be happy to know that I kept it safe for you and never once opened it," Greta said in a rush of breath, almost too fast for Martha to follow. As the two women sat together in the parlor, their eyes locked as Martha tried to process everything Greta had said and done for her, and Greta prayed that Martha wouldn't be angry with her. In fact, Martha couldn't help but laugh.

"My dear, Mrs. Royal, I just can't believe this!" Martha said, taking the saddlebag as Greta pushed towards her. Martha unclasped the buckle and peered inside. The mounds of cash were still there as though she'd never parted with them.

"Are you angry, Miss Walters?" Greta asked after a while, wondering if the large smile on Martha's face was a true sign of how she was feeling.

"No, Mrs. Royal, I'm not angry with you at all. You have done the kindest thing imaginable for me. I don't know how I can ever repay you," Martha said, feeling overjoyed and overwhelmed at the same time. She'd never expected to see this money again.

"Well, let's just not tell Bill that I took it from your room, or I'm afraid he'd have to fire me," Greta said, so seriously that Martha couldn't help but laugh again. She pulled the older woman into a tight hug, doing her best not to squeal in delight so she didn't wake Lucy.

"You must stay for dinner, Mrs. Royal. I will make you

whatever you wish and we shall have tea and cake while we wait," Martha said enthusiastically as she slung the saddlebag over her shoulder and led Greta to the kitchen, intent on treating her like a queen that day. Greta simply chuckled as she followed the young lady, unable to deny her.

EPILOGUE

Martha was trying to keep her composure as Lucy fanned both their faces at the same time with extra pew fans they'd found in the pastor's office. They were waiting for Sam to meeting them in the room to let them know that the wedding was about to begin.

"I can't believe it, Lucy. It all still feels like I'm living in a dream and I'm afraid that at any moment I'm going to wake up," Martha said as she took deep breaths to settle her nerves.

"Ye have nothing to feel nervous about, Martha. Gray is lucky to have ya as a wife. Ye are everything a man could want in a woman, and a whole bunch more," Lucy said enthusiastically, even though the heat of the day was starting to get to her. "Where in the world is that husband of mine?"

As though Sam had been waiting to be summoned, he opened the door in the next moment as the "Wedding March" began to play. "Who's ready to marry a feisty ranch hand?" Sam said with a smile, causing the ladies to chuckle.

"Behave, ye," Lucy said as she walked past her husband carrying a small bouquet of roses. She looked radiant in a pale green gown that made her pregnant figure very flattering, especially with its layers of lace. Lucy gave Martha a wink as she stepped out of the room and down the aisle of the church, heading towards the altar, where Gray stood with Bright Star and Josh at his side.

"You look beautiful, Martha," Sam said, his voice taking on a serious note. "Gray is truly lucky to have a woman like you."

Martha beamed up at Sam, so happy that he'd agreed to walk her down the aisle, after everything he'd done for her and Gray. After all, it was he who told Gray about her arrival, which had been perfect, since her last letter had never arrived in Spruce Valley. "It is I who is lucky, Sam. After everything I went through to arrive to this moment, I am lucky to even be alive," Martha said, turning her eyes back to the open door. Just a little further down the aisle and she'd be able to see Gray.

"Well then, let's get you married so you can begin the rest of your life as Mrs. Jenkins," Sam said with a smile. Martha simply nodded as she allowed Sam to guide her forward.

Gray was standing at the front of the church, his heart pounding in his chest as the wedding music had begun. With the entire town appearing to have shown up for the occasion, the building was rather warm, and he was afraid to ruin his new suit by sweating too much. He took deep breaths, his eyes forward as he waited to catch sight of his bride.

He couldn't believe how much he'd come to love Martha, even when she didn't have a penny to her name. And then, what seemed like a moment later, she had become one of the wealthiest women in the area. It was only to him that she had confessed what Greta had done with the stolen money and how the older woman had returned it to her. The news had been so unreal, that if it hadn't been for Martha showing him the money, he would have never believed it. Together, with their two fortunes, they were able to have a decent-sized house built down the lane from the ranch. It was close enough to the ranch for Gray's work, and Martha could continue working with Lucy; but Martha would also be a little bit closer to town so she could run their new women's boutique.

Gray had also taken the time to finally tell Martha the truth about why he'd left England. As a member of a wealthy family, he'd been expected to run the family business after his father died, but he'd run away from home to marry a young lady who had captured his heart. But when this lady only showed interest in his money, and since he'd lost his inheritance when he'd chosen to elope with her, she'd left in minutes after he'd explained their future prospects. Heartbroken, and now penniless after being raised a very wealthy person, he'd fled to the Americas to make his fortune, intent on never loving again.

Gray's own story of love and betrayal had brought him and Martha closer together, allowing him to feel that it was finally the right time to propose. The night before Martha and Lucy's boutique had opened, Gray had surprised Martha at the shop and knelt before her, offering up his heart and a small token of his affection: a beautiful silver ring with diamonds embedded in the band. Martha had been surprised and overjoyed by Gray's proposal, and when they shared the good news with the

Slaters, Lucy had insisted on making Martha's gown, even this late on in her pregnancy.

Now, Gray looked ahead as Sam and Martha came into sight, but Gray only had eyes for his bride. Dressed in a gorgeous flowing white gown, Martha appeared to be an angel coming his way. It fit her figure perfectly despite her growing stomach; her auburn hair was done up in an intricate design with pins embossed with pearls. Pearls decorated the front of the gown as well, making her shine before him.

"Who presents this young lady to this man?" Reverend Paul said as Sam placed Martha's hands in Gray's.

"The Slaters," Sam replied, winking at Gray before he went to join his wife in the pew.

Martha and Gray stared into each other's eyes as they tried to listen to the Reverend's words, but they became more focused on the feeling of their hands together, and their eyes, which were locked in a state of love and adoration. When a soft chuckle rang through the air, Gray refocused and had the Reverend repeat the vows so he could say them correctly. Martha did the same, and as Reverend Paul introduced them to the attendees, Gray was quick to draw Martha to him and give her a long, passionate kiss that received many hoots and hollers from the crowd.

Leading his wife down the aisle to the open church doors, Gray couldn't believe that the time had finally come for him to take that step in life where he'd become a husband, and perhaps one day a father. Though he had a few grey hairs, he knew that his age wouldn't stop him from loving Martha ever day as though that day was their last.

AFTER A WARM RECEPTION at the Eatery, Martha and Gray returned to their home, the first time either one of them would be sleeping in the new place. Having worked with Zachariah Welliver, the local furniture maker, they had everything they needed to enjoy their first night together as a married couple.

As tradition requires, as soon as Gray had stopped the buggy out front, he'd helped Martha down and then gathered her into his arms, carrying her over the threshold of their new home. "Welcome home, Mrs. Jenkins," he said, setting her down and pulling her into a lingering kiss.

"Why, thank you, Mr. Jenkins," Martha said before kissing him back, loving the way his strong arms wrapped around her.

"How about you go get comfortable upstairs and I'll put Chestnut in the barn," Gray said, his voice husky as he placed a kiss on her forehead.

"Okay," Martha said shyly as she finally let go of her husband. He stood there a moment, simply watching his wife in her beautiful gown, before heading back outside to take care of the mare.

Gray couldn't believe how lucky he was to have a woman like Martha in his life. Though they'd overcome much together by confessing their own histories to each other, Gray couldn't deny that he felt a love for Martha unlike anything he'd ever felt before. He worked quick with settling Chestnut for the night so he could return to his loving wife.

As Martha waited for Gray to meet her in their room, she took her time looking around, slowly taking the pins from her hair and laying them down on the dresser that was across from the four-poster bed. Everything felt so new to her that it almost seemed that none of it was real. She sighed as her hair was finally free of all the pins, allowing her to relax a bit. But as she tried to unbutton her gown by herself, hoping to be in her sleeping gown by the time Gray returned, she began to get frustrated.

Hearing his footsteps coming down the hallway, she stopped struggling, knowing that she would have to wait for his help. Her heart began to race as Gray approached their bedroom door, and she knew that she was about to face the rest of her life with this man, in their new home, starting in their own bedroom. For a moment, Martha could envision the rest of their lives together: having children, raising them together, watching them grow up, and then growing old together. Martha was smiling even before Gray came into the room, creating a beautiful scene for him to see as he stepped into their room.

With her long auburn hair flowing down her back, Martha looked even more gorgeous to Gray. She looked wild, but more importantly, she looked happy. Without speaking, Gray went to her, collecting her in his arms as he kissed her fondly. After a moment, as they both became very warm, Gray looked into Martha's eyes and said, "Mrs. Martha Jenkins. For the rest of my days on this Earth, I will always love you. And every night, no matter what the day has brought, we will come to this room together, united, of sound mind and of one love."

"Gray, I look forward to our life together. I look forward to the sound of small feet on the floor, days spent around the kitchen table laughing and playing with our children – but I also look forward to the years we simply spend together, just the two of us," Martha said, running her fingers through his hair, loving the feeling of being so close to him for the rest of her life.

Gray lowered his head to her then, capturing her in a kiss that would represent their strong love for each other, and the many promises left untold that would help pave the way for their happy future together – no matter what happened next.

The End

CAST OF CHARACTERS

MARTHA WALTERS/ MARY CARVER

- **Gray Jenkins**
- Jared Mathews, Martha's ex-fiancé
- Max, villain of the story
- Sheriff Josh Ryder
- Bill Eckert, owner of the Honeywell Inn
- Greta Royal, widow and housekeeper
- Mayor Delphina Stavros
- Elena, Delphina's daughter
- Reverend Paul & Annette Gibbons
- Drake, Ernie's eldest son
- Robert, Drake's brother
- Nell, waitress at the Eatery
- Zachariah Welliver, furniture maker
- Jensen Davis, ranch hand
- Tom Barker, ranch hand
- Eddie & Sawyer Murtaugh, brothers

AMELIA'S OTHER BOOKS

Montana Westward Brides series

#0 The Rancher's Fiery Bride

#1 The Reckless Doctor's Bride

#2 The Rancher's Unexpected Pregnant Bride

#3 The Lonesome Cowboy's Abducted Bride

#4 The Sheriff's Stubborn Secretive Bride

CONNECT WITH AMELIA

Visit my website at **www.ameliarose.info** to view my other books and to sign up to my mailing list so that you are notified about my new releases and special offers.

ABOUT AMELIA ROSE

Amelia is a shameless romance addict with no intentions of ever kicking the habit. Growing up she dreamed of entertaining people and taking them on fantastical journeys with her acting abilities, until she came to the realization as a college sophomore that she had none to speak of. Another ten years would pass before she discovered a different means to accomplishing the same dream: writing stories of love and passion for addicts just like herself. Amelia has always loved romance stories and she tries to tie all the elements she likes about them into her writing.

Made in the USA
Middletown, DE
21 May 2023

31105086R00109